Colin

The McClains

Kirsten Osbourne

Chapter One

Colin McClain hated training. So, he rarely participated. He was considered too valuable to his clan to be killed anyway. Normally his brother Blake took care of the training of the men because he had an incredible ability when it came to warfare. Blake could move objects and people with his mind. In the middle of a battle, he could move a huge boulder onto their adversaries, and that was something that would be very useful in war.

In the McClain family, every seventh son had seven sons, and every seventh son had a power that made them the future laird of the clan. Colin was the seventh son of his generation, but his wasn't the same as the others. Each of Colin's brothers had a different power. Colin, as the youngest, was the last to show a power, and to everyone's surprise, he had the powers of all six of his brothers.

No one was quite sure what had happened with this generation, but his great-grandmother, Beth, had said it probably had something to do with Colin being part of the seventh generation of McClains since they'd developed powers. It was very confusing to most people, but Colin and his brothers all knew it would be best if they simply didn't show their powers to people who were not part of their immediate family.

Colin had escaped from the keep by going for a walk, even though he knew he should be participating in the training that was happening. Anyone else would have been considered less than smart for going out and walking so far from the keep, but the combination of powers Colin possessed, made him a great deal more self-sufficient than most people.

As he walked, he thought about how little he wanted to be the future laird of his clan. He would take over from his father when he married, so he planned to keep from marrying for as long as possible, though his father and mother were urging him in the direction his brothers had taken.

Something caught the corner of his eye, and he watched for a moment, trying to see exactly what it was. It seemed to be a woman, in English dress. He walked toward her, looking around and seeing no one else. She had a blindfold over her eyes, and her hands were tied behind her back.

He used his speed to be at her side in a moment. Speed was the power he shared with his brother Finn. He could transport himself to anywhere he could see as well, but transportation made him feel more vulnerable than super speed did.

He removed her blindfold and cut through the rope that bound her hands together. Her wrists were raw. "Are ye all right, lass?"

She blinked against the bright sunlight. "I think so. Where are the men who took me from my father?"

Colin carefully looked in every direction, unable to sense anyone near them. "I believe ye are alone."

"Ugh! I told them my father wouldn't pay their ransom! They took me from my home just south of Hadrian's Wall and forced me to come with them. I begged them to return me. I'm the youngest of eight daughters. My father won't pay a ransom. Instead, he'll be happy there's one less dowry to pay."

Colin reached down to help her to her feet. "What's your name?"

"Does it matter? I have had no chaperon for days. I'm certain my life is ruined no matter what my name is. You may as well call me Jezebel." There were tears in the beautiful woman's blue eyes, and he longed to help her.

"I willna call ye that. I am Colin McClain. The walk to my family's land is not far."

"I'm Brynna, daughter of the Earl of Hereford." Brynna shook her head. "I'm the least important of all my father's daughters. He hasn't even looked for a husband for me, and I'm nearing twenty summers!"

"Would you care to take refuge with the Clan McClain. I know my father, the laird, would allow you room and board as you find a suitable mate. If that is not to your liking, I can arrange for a contingent of men to take you back to England and your father."

"You would help me this way?" she asked, sounding surprised.

"Aye, I would. But if I may, I will see to your wounds first." He pulled a small glass bottle with a cork in it from his pocket and rubbed the water in the bottle over her wrists. As he did, he applied his power of healing, and her wrists were immediately healed.

"What is in that bottle?" she asked. "Tis a miracle!"

He smiled. "I am a healer. I carry medicines in case I find an injured person." He offered his arm. "Whether you go back to England or stay in Scotland, the first step is to return to my keep and my family's lands."

She took the arm. "Do you have water with you?" she asked. "I have had nothing to drink for a good long time. I don't know how long they left me tied up that way. I know twas after they received word my father would not pay their ransom."

He took his waterskin from his side and handed it to her. "Drink your fill. Tis only an hour's walk home."

"My legs are cramped terribly. I know not if I can walk all that way." She drank greedily from the water.

He pulled some dried meat from his pouch and gave it to her as well. "If ye haven't had water then I'm sure ye haven't had any food."

"Your speech is odd. At times you sound like a highlander, but at others, you sound like you are from a faraway place."

He smiled. "When ye meet my mother, you will understand."

"All right," she said, eyeing him curiously. "I don't think I can make it that far."

He sighed. "I'll carry you. I can move very quickly, but ye must close yer eyes or ye will get sick."

She blinked a few times. "On foot, you think you can carry me fast enough that I would be sick? Tis impossible."

"Nay, it isn't. We will be home in less than two minutes if you will but allow me to hold you and close your eyes."

Brynna laughed. "Colin, you are a funny man. I'll play your game." She closed her eyes tightly, and he lifted her into his arms.

Colin smiled. He liked this lass, no matter who she was. Holding her tightly, he used his speed and stopped beside the keep of the Clan McClain. "Here we are, Brynna."

She opened her eyes and her jaw dropped. "How did you move so quickly?" she asked.

"I'm very fast," Colin replied. "Come inside. This is my home, where I will live with my parents until I marry and inherit the title laird from my father."

"Laird?" she asked, surprised. She knew the title was similar to being an earl in England.

He had a firm grip on her hand as he led her into the keep, calling out for his mother. She came out of the parlor, looking at him curiously. "This is Brynna. She was taken from her father's home in England, with the hope her father would pay a ransom for her. When he refused, she was left tied up and blindfolded."

"Oh, that's terrible! You must be both exhausted and famished."

Brynna smiled, immediately curtsying to the woman, who she knew must be the current Lady McClain. "It's a pleasure to meet you." Her gesture was lost when her shaking legs gave way and she fell into a heap on the floor.

"Oh, dear!" Lady McClain glared at her son. "Carry her to one of the bedrooms upstairs. I'll alert the kitchen to send a tray of food and water."

Colin didn't need to be told twice. He swooped Brynna up into his arms and carried her up the staircase to a bedroom that appeared to be uninhabited. He carefully set her on the bed, stepping back as he knew his mother would follow immediately after speaking with the kitchen.

"Are you all right, lass?" he asked again.

Brynna sighed. "I'm much worse than I thought. My legs feel as if they're made of water."

"May I use my special healing potion on them?"

She nodded gratefully. "That would help a great deal if you have enough."

"I can always make more," he said. "I will have to touch your bare legs."

She frowned but nodded. Modesty couldn't bother her when he was a healer. She lifted her torn, dirty dress until it was just above her knees.

He poured a generous amount of water into his hand and healed her legs as he was rubbing them. "Now, is anything else injured?"

"I'm just hungry and thirsty and I need sleep."

"Aye. My mother will take care of those things in a moment or two."

When his mother walked in a second later, her skirts were still rucked up above her knees, and she blushed. "He was healing me."

Lady McClain smiled. "I understand. My son is an excellent healer, isn't he?"

"He is," Brynna said. "He could sell the potions he makes for a great deal of money."

"My son doesn't heal to become rich. He heals because it helps others. Just as he helped you today." Lady McClain frowned. "What will you do? Will you go home to your father? Or choose a mate from our clan?"

Brynna's eyes widened. "Colin said he would send me home with a contingent of men if I chose."

"Absolutely. You need to choose what's best for you."

Brynna looked at Colin with his dark hair and eyes. There was just something about him. "I choose Colin," she said, though she knew she had no place saying it.

Lady McClain clapped delightedly. "Well, Colin?"

Colin looked at the beautiful girl he'd found and thought about what it would mean to be married to her. He would immediately become laird, and she would need to learn his secrets. He wasn't certain if he was ready for either thing, but he understood the lass wouldn't be able to trust many men after she'd been left the way she had.

"Aye, I'll marry her. But she needs a few days to rest first."

Lady McClain smiled happily. She looked at Brynna. "You've made me the happiest woman alive."

"Colin will need to talk to you about some odd things about our family, and if you're still agreeable after, we'll start talking about what we'll have for your wedding feast." Lady McClain left the room and closed the door firmly behind her.

Colin pulled a chair from the corner of the room to sit at Brynna's bedside. "Before I tell you this, I need your word you will tell no one, even if you decide to go home to England."

Brynna frowned. "You have my word."

"There are seven sons in my family, and I am the youngest. When I marry, I will sire seven sons. There will be no daughters. Every seventh son has seven sons. And the seventh son always has a power." He took a deep breath, watching her face to see if she looked skeptical.

"What do you mean by a power?" she asked.

He pulled the potion he'd used on her from his pocket, handing her the bottle. "'Tis water," he said softly.

"Water? But that can't be!"

"Have you any scars on your body that never really healed?" he asked.

She nodded, showing him a spot above her left eyebrow. "I was playing with my sister, and I fell onto a rock. It never healed properly."

"Put your finger on the scar. Feel it."

She did as he asked, wondering why he was having her touch the scar. It had been a part of her for so long, she did not remember a time when she didn't have it. "I am touching it."

"Can you feel where your skin dips in?" If this didn't work, Colin knew he could fetch one of his mother's twenty-first century mirrors, but he also knew just the sight of it would be frightening.

"Yes, of course." Brynna was starting to think the man had lost his mind.

He put his hand over hers and healed the scar. When he removed his hand, he asked, "Can you feel it now?"

Brynna tried to find the scar with her fingers, but it seemed to have disappeared. "'Tis gone."

"I have the power to heal," he said softly. He'd give her a minute to let that sink in before he told her of his other five powers.

"And every seventh son in your family can heal?" she asked.

"Nay. My father can command animals. My grandfather can feel the emotions of people around him. My great-grandfather was a healer as I am. His father could move his hand inside of things."

"Inside of things?" Brynna asked, confused.

"He can move his hand through a wall." Colin said it casually, as if it was just normal for a man to have a power.

She shook her head. "I think I'm starting to see things. I have been awake too long."

"You can sleep, but we'll just have to have the entire conversation again tomorrow," Colin said with a smile.

"Why wouldn't I want to marry a man who can heal people with a touch?" she asked finally.

"Because you would have to bear seven sons, and you wouldn't be given the option of daughters. You could have granddaughters, but not daughters."

She frowned. "I know men prefer a family with no daughters, and I'd rather not bear any. I won't let them be forgotten as I have been."

There was a knock at the door, and Cook, the mistress of the kitchen, brought in a tray with bread, meat, and cheese, as well as a large glass of water. "Here ye are, lass."

"Thank you," Brynna said softly. No matter how often her family had told her she didn't need to thank the servants, she couldn't seem to stop. It was about being polite.

The woman smiled at her, nodding once, and exiting the room.

"That was Cook. She has been here since before I was born, and her mother was the cook before her. When you are mistress of the keep, you will be the one to instruct her in her duties."

Brynna frowned. "The oldest son inherits when his father dies, correct?"

"You would think so... No in my family, the youngest son takes on the title of laird when he marries. Then his father will be there to advise him when it is necessary." Colin shrugged. "My mother told you there were odd things about our family."

"Why do you talk strangely? Your mother does as well." She asked between bites of the food in front of her. As hungry as she was, she had to make sure her mouth was empty before she spoke.

"This is where the story of my family turns strange," he said.

Brynna's eyes widened. "The rest you've told me has *not* been strange?"

Colin grinned. "My mother, my aunt, my grandmother, and my great-grandmother have all come back in time from the twenty-first century. They have amazing books and strange devices they can show you so that you will know they are telling the truth. But they are from a land across the ocean. A land that will not be discovered for another one hundred-twenty years."

Brynna started laughing. She couldn't help it. "They are future women, are they?"

Colin smiled. "It's true, and you'll see that what I've said is the total truth. I'll let my mother convince you of her time travel tomorrow. For now, you should just finish eating and sleep."

"Will you really marry me if I decide that's what I want?"

He nodded. "My parents believe I've been derelict in my duties for not marrying yet. You are a pretty girl, and one whom I would gladly take as my wife."

"Then I'll decide. I believe you about your family. It's strange, but you showed me it was true. Your mother coming back in time is too much of a stretch of the imagination for me."

"I understand," he said, sitting with her while she finished eating. She was going to be surprised by his other powers because he couldn't tell her absolutely everything until she believed what he'd told her already.

Chapter Two

When Brynna woke the following morning, she looked around her. The previous day, nay the previous fortnight, had to have been a dream. Though the previous day had been different from the rest of the dream.

But she was in the room where Colin had put her, and where she'd eaten, and fallen asleep with him in a chair beside her bed. She looked to the chair, which was still there, but empty now. She wanted to sit up and yell for him to help her, but she truly didn't need help. She needed to know what she was supposed to do. Waking up in a keep in another country wasn't how she'd planned to spend her day.

Finally, she decided to call out and see if anyone came to her. "Hello!" she bellowed, knowing it was unladylike, and at that moment, not caring.

The door opened quickly. "Are you all right, lass?" Colin stood there, looking at her quizzingly.

"I didn't know what I was supposed to do now."

He nodded. "I will inform my mother you are awake. She will see to a bath for you and clothes that are not rags."

Brynna immediately felt ashamed of her appearance. She put a hand to her hair, and she could feel leaves and sticks. Why on earth had the man agreed to marry her with her being so disheveled?

"Thank you."

Colin walked closer and took the chair beside her. "Don't be embarrassed, lass. Tis not your fault you look as you do. I'll get the description of your abductors from you, and an army will be sent to deal with them."

"No, Colin!" Brynna shook her head adamantly. "I don't want to join your clan as the person they are warring over. Let me put it behind me."

He nodded. "If that is truly your wish, that is what will be done." Though it went against his every instinct, he would do as she asked. He was not a warrior by nature, and he had no desire to start a war, but he did want to avenge Brynna. It was a war within his mind, and he was not happy about it.

"You said your mother will be the one helping me find clothing and get cleaned up. Where will you be?" Brynna asked.

Collin smiled. "I'll be close by. If you feel nervous or need me to come to you, just think very loudly, 'I need you, Colin,' and I'll be here."

"How can a person think loudly?" she asked, looking almost as confused as she felt.

Colin smiled, stroking her cheek, which was covered in dirt, but he knew he shouldn't say anything to her about it. She was already embarrassed about how she looked. "I don't know how to describe it, but I can promise you, it will work!"

Brynna shook her head at him. "You are going to be a very strange husband, aren't you?"

He chuckled. "Wait and see." He stood. "I'll fetch my mother now and leave the two of you alone. I'm certain you don't want me to watch you bathe and try on a new dress."

Brynna blushed and shooed him away with one hand. Being married to Colin would be wonderful—all she'd ever hoped for and more. She didn't fancy herself in love with the man, but he was strong and kind. Her mother told her once that was the only thing a lady could ask for in a man.

Lady McClain was in her room moments later. "I had Cook save some breakfast for you, and your bathwater is being heated as we speak." She set the tray she was carrying on the bed beside Brynna, who sat up and began to happily eat the food on the tray. It had been much too long since she'd eaten her fill. Last night seemed to have barely touched her hunger.

"Thank you," Brynna said as she stuffed food into her mouth.

"I brought something with me for you to see. Colin told me you don't believe I'm from the future, and I probably wouldn't either if I were in your shoes."

Brynna looked down at her feet, which were bare. Her slippers had been shredded as she'd walked along behind the hideous men who had taken her. "I'm not wearing shoes."

Lady McClain laughed. "It's an expression from the future." She pulled something from her pocket that looked odd to Brynna. It was a rectangle made of metal. "This is what I want to show you." She handed the object to Brynna.

"What is it?" Brynna asked, turning the thing over in her hands.

"It's a telephone. It doesn't let you talk to people here, which is one of the reasons to have the device but look." Lady McClain reached over and moved her finger over the rectangle, and it showed a picture that had not been there before. "I use this for reading books."

"You read?" Brynna asked. She'd always wanted to learn, but her father had said reading was unladylike, and she'd not been given the opportunity to learn.

"I do. I'll teach you if you'd like."

Brynna's eyes lit up. "Oh, Lady McClain! I can think of nothing I would enjoy more!"

"Please, call me Holli."

"Holli then," Brynna said. "But first I must be cleaned. I cannot touch books with as filthy as I am."

Holli smiled. "No, you cannot. I thought about insisting you bathe last night, but you simply weren't up to it. I could see on your face how much you needed to sleep."

"I am still very tired," Brynna said. "But I am not a laze about!"

Holli laughed. "I never thought you were. Do you believe I'm from the future now?"

Brynna shrugged. "I believe that you *think* you are from the future. I will reserve judgment about my own beliefs."

"You are a wise woman," Holli said. "Would you like to see naked baby pictures of Colin?"

"What is a picture?"

Holli pursed her lips, obviously trying to find the right words to explain it. "A picture is something that preserves the memory of something perfectly." She took the device Brynna held, and tapped it a few times, and then handed it back.

When Brynna looked at it, there was a baby who had no clothes on, lying on the floor. "Is this Colin?"

"It is. I've been saving that picture since he was a baby so I could show it to the woman he'd marry." Holli looked particularly proud of herself.

"Do you do this to tease him?"

Holli nodded emphatically. "So, you need to tell him when you see him again that you saw him naked."

Brynna laughed. "He said I could call to him in my mind, and he would hear me."

"He will. Think to him what you want to say, and don't be surprised if you hear him speak back."

Brynna closed her eyes and thought, "You do not look very manly in the pictures your mother has shown me. She called them naked baby pictures."

It only took a moment before she heard a groan. "I can't believe she actually showed you that. She's been telling me she would my whole life."

Brynna giggled. "I did feel as if he was speaking to me. How does he do that?"

"That power is called telepathy," Holli said. "He only uses it with family, but as you are about to become his wife, I knew he would be listening for you." She grinned at Brynna. "Did he sound annoyed?"

"He did. I feel like I shouldn't have looked. Will he use a heavy hand with me?"

Holli's eyes widened. "Will he hit you, you mean?"

Brynna nodded. "I know my father was heavier-handed with my mother than he should have been. He left bruises on her arms and face quite often. We all hid from him when he was into his cups."

"If my son ever hits you for any reason, you are to come straight to me. He was raised to help ladies, not to hurt them."

Brynna's eyes widened. "But all men discipline their wives—especially when they're into their cups."

"No, not all men do. My husband has never struck me, and I know my father-in-law has never struck his wife either. You must tell me if it ever happens, and I will personally deal with my son." Holli continued to mumble under her breath for a moment.

Brynna thought she heard something about giving an abusive man a bowl of Earl's black-eyed peas, but she didn't know which earl she was talking about or what black-eyed peas were.

A servant knocked at the door then, carrying in a bathtub, and a stream of servants came behind the first, each carrying a bucket of hot water. The bath was filled, and Brynna finished eating quickly. A bath sounded quite heavenly.

"My father said women should only take baths in the spring, and then only once each year. I'm thankful that you're allowing me a second bath this year."

"I take a bath every day," Holli replied. "The servants here think it's odd, but they don't mind. I'm sure they'll fill a bath for you every day as well."

"I will feel like I'm living the life of a queen!" Brynna responded, waiting for the last servant to leave. She stood up, thankful that her legs felt like they would hold her again, and she quickly undressed.

"Do you want me to wash your hair for you?" Holli asked.

"Oh, yes! I would love that." Usually, a servant saw to her bathing needs, but as long as it was another woman, Brynna didn't mind.

While she sat in the tub, Holli washed her hair, and handed her a cloth so she could wash herself. Then Holli began the long, tedious process of brushing Brynna's hair.

"I don't know if you'll ever be able to get all the snarls out," Brynna said. "We may have to cut it off."

"Do you want to cut it off? Or do you like it long?"

"It is meant to be long," Brynna said. "Hair is the most important part of a woman's beauty."

"I don't think my son will agree with you on that, though you do have beautiful hair. I wondered what color it would be once the dirt was gone. It's very pretty."

"I hope that Colin thinks the same." Brynna leaned her head forward so Holli could get to the knots at the back of her neck. "Do you think he feels trapped by my suggesting the two of us marry?"

"If he did, he wouldn't have agreed to it. My son has refused a great deal of ladies in the past few years. He is pleased with you. I could see it on his face."

"Even though I looked like I had been dragged through mud?"

Holli laughed softly. "I don't think he felt that way."

Finally, her hair was brushed out, but Brynna's bath was already cold. "I'm getting wrinkles all over me," she said with a laugh. "I must get out. I'd love to see the keep."

"I guess you didn't get a chance to see much. Did you see the loch?"

Brynna shook her head. "No. I was unable to walk here so Colin held me and told me to close my eyes. And then we were here. I know not how he did it."

"He has two powers that would have allowed him to bring you here while your eyes were closed. I believe he probably used his super speed because he is more comfortable with that than teleporting."

"What is...teleporting?" Brynna was becoming more and more amazed with this man she was marrying by the minute.

"Did he not tell you about his powers?" Holli asked.

"He told me he could heal people with a touch. Does he have others?"

Holli sighed. "This was the seventh generation of McClain men with powers. And this generation had all seven brothers having power. The first six had a single power each, but Colin...Colin got each of their powers."

Brynna allowed Holli to help her into a shift before responding. "Why would he not tell me?"

"Probably because you disbelieved him about me coming from the future. He decided you had heard enough at that point, and he'd tell you more later." Holli shook her head. "He's always been difficult."

Brynna frowned. "I'm going to have to ask him about all of his powers."

"Yes, you are. He will join us for the noon meal, I am certain, and then I will send the two of you on a walk around the loch. You'll love it, and you can make him tell you everything."

"All right," Brynna said softly. She thought loudly, "You didn't tell me everything. I have to hear things from your mother?"

Colin thought back to her, "I worried it was too much for you to hear all at once. I will explain all to you this afternoon."

"Yes, you will," she thought back, feeling more than a little perturbed with the man. She was glad now she'd seen his naked baby picture. He should be embarrassed for not telling her everything.

She would tell him exactly how that made her feel as they went on their walk.

Chapter Three

After their noon meal, during which Brynna met Colin's father, Colin and Brynna went out to walk around the loch. It was early autumn, but already the air was nippy. As soon as they were away from his parents, Brynna said, "You should have been the one to tell me about all your powers. I thought you could only heal, but your mother explained everything to me."

Colin looked sheepish for a moment, rubbing the back of his neck. "I meant to. But when I told ye me mother was from the future, and ye didna believe me, I thought it best to tell you about one power at a time."

She glared at him. "I felt guilty after seeing your naked baby picture and finding out you were embarrassed. Then I found out you'd only told me a little bit of what I needed to know, and I decided I shouldn't feel guilty. The naked picture was my due."

Colin sighed. "I'm sorry, lass. I never meant ta upset ye!"

"I know that too. It does make me trust you less though. Mayhap we should put the wedding off until I know ye better."

He caught her arm and stopped walking. "We can't."

She put her hands on her hips and glared at him. "And why not?"

"My mother has already made plans for our wedding feast which will happen two days hence."

"I'm sure she can postpone them."

"I dinna want her to." He reached out and pulled her toward him, kissing her softly. "I am ready for the wedding night."

Her lips tingled from the brief kiss. "Is that so?"

"It is." He rested his hands on her hips and leaned down to kiss her once more. This kiss was the opposite of the one before. This was a long, deep kiss that had her legs turn shaky.

"I did not say you could kiss me."

"You've agreed to marry me. That's permission to kiss."

"You have made my legs shaky, and I want no more of that."

He smirked down at her, kissing her once more. "I want your whole body shaking in me arms."

Brynna's eyes widened and she stared at him. "Colin...I think we need a little more time to get to know one another."

He shook his head. "Tis not going to happen. Me mother has already had the cooks start to make all of the family's favorite foods."

"And what are these favorite foods? What if I don't like them?"

"Oh, you'll love them. We'll have tacos, and Irish nachos."

"Irish?" She bit back the desire to tell him that Irish was as bad as Scotland in that both countries had men running around wild.

"Yes, it's something my mother and grandmother and aunt brought back with them from the twenty-first century. It's a delicious treat that you will love."

"I see. You cannot tell me more about it?"

He shook his head. "Many of the ingredients won't be discovered until the new world, which won't be discovered for over a century yet. I know tis odd, but they brought seeds from that new land to grow things that won't be found here for another two-hundred years or so."

"Why would they do that?" she asked, her brow furrowed.

"Because they wanted to marry highlanders, but they didn't want to give up their favorite foods, I guess. My mother is always talking about how much she misses root beer, whatever that may be."

"Mayhap a beer made from roots and not from barley?"

He shrugged. "Possibly. We'll probably never know for certain."

He offered his arm to her, and they continued their walk. She wasn't certain why she enjoyed kissing the man when he'd deliberately kept things from her, but she liked it, nevertheless. "Will I get any say in what's served?" she asked.

"If you would like one. Talk to Mother. She'll tell you what she's planned and ask if you'd like something added to it. You should ask her for brownies."

"What is that?" she asked.

"You'll see. And you'll never be the same again after you've tasted them."

"I will only believe it once I've tasted them. Whatever they may be."

"On the day of our wedding, my parents will move into one of the cottages in the village. Tis the opposite of how most clans do things, but it's the way our clan has always done it."

She frowned. "Your parents should not lose their home simply because we marry!"

"I agree, but they will both say they've been laird and lady for too long, and they would like to have fewer responsibilities. Tis strange, but apparently that's what all the lairds say when the youngest son takes power."

His clan's way of doing things seemed very odd to her, but she supposed they could do things the way they wanted to do them. "Will your mother give me advice if I ask for it?"

"Of course! Father and Mother will both be there to help us with anything we need. Tis a small part of the reason the clan does things the way they do. Then the former laird and lady are able to help as the new laird and lady take their place." Colin grinned at her. She was starting to seem to like the idea of marrying in just two days. "You don't mind bearing seven children?"

She frowned. "No one can predict how many children will be born."

"Tis always been the way with my family since well before the Norman conquest of England. My family came from Normandy."

"They did not want to stay in their own country?"

"From the stories I've been told of my ancestors, most of the family did stay in Normandy, but one seventh son came here with William the Conqueror, and my family has grown from that seventh son. He brought the luck with him, and he had seven sons, and the youngest had seven sons. It's a good way to grow a family quickly."

"Your brother's wives won't have seven sons? Even though your brothers have powers as well?"

Colin shook his head. "They will not. Already four of them have daughters. It's my burden to carry on the line with seven sons. Mine and yours."

Brynna sighed. "I still am not sure I believe I will bear seven sons." It seemed too outrageous for her to believe.

"You must believe soon. I promise, seven sons will be all we have. No daughters."

"Your mother said the same, and still, I have trouble believing."

"Having grown up believing seven sons are normal, I have no trouble believing." He realized only then they had walked all the way around the loch. "I should take you back to my mother, so you can help her with wedding plans."

"I fear that she would not like for me to disagree with plans she's already made." She bit her lip. "Your mother has promised to teach me to read. Would that bother you?"

"If you could read?" He shook his head. "Of course not. I think if anyone wants to learn to read, they should be taught. Many of my aunts learned to read from my mother and grandmother. Not everyone in the village can read, but a fair number can thanks to their efforts."

"Would I be allowed to teach our children to read then?"

"Yes. Most definitely yes. All of my brothers and I can read. And I know my aunt has taught all of my brothers' wives. They even loan out their strange devices that have books on them, though there are no pages to turn. I have no idea why they think what is on them are books, but they will stare at the screen of these devices for hours whenever they get the chance."

It was all Brynna could do not to squeal with delight. She loved the idea of being taught to read, and no one being kept from the same knowledge. This village would be an educated one. She was happy to be part of it.

Colin walked with her back to the keep, and he left her with his mother, who was sitting in the parlor with one of her strange devices. Holli looked up as they walked into the keep. "Oh, good! You brought Brynna back to me. I want to go over what I plan to serve at the wedding feast with her."

Colin leaned down and kissed Brynna's cheek. "I will be looking in on each home and making sure no one is ill."

Holli nodded. "We want to stop any illness as soon as it creeps into our village." She turned to look at Brynna who had taken the seat beside her. "Once Colin is laird, then his brother will be the one calling on everyone in the village each day. Sometimes we don't hear about an illness until someone is already dead, and we would prefer to heal all."

"Which brother can heal?" Brynna asked. She knew she'd been told, but as she hadn't met a single one of the brothers, it was hard for her to remember who went with which power.

"Archie can heal. I thought I'd messed something up with the family when all the boys were born with powers. Colin was three before he revealed his powers to me, and I was very concerned." Holli shook her head. "The boys all knew, and they thought it was fun to keep the secret."

"So all the boys worked together to fool you? That was not kind of them!"

"No, but they all love me, and I love them. It was a very long time ago."

"I'm certain. Colin mentioned Irish nachuse and something called pacos?"

"Irish nachos and tacos. I serve them for all the big events, but I want you to try them before I commit to them. Cook is making both for supper tonight and another favorite of mine called shepherd's pie. You'll get a small portion of each, and you can let me know what you think of them, and we can do all three for the wedding feast or just one or two."

"Colin said I must also try something called brownies?"

Holli smiled. "I have those planned for dessert. It's going to be a fun meal!"

"It sounds as if it will." Brynna frowned. "Colin said the wedding will be two days hence?"

Holli nodded. "We're not going to make the two of you wait. Obviously, you have feelings for my boy, and he has them for you."

Brynna bit her lip. "I chose him because I trusted him, and now I'm not as certain I can trust him. He didn't tell me everything."

"He would have before the wedding. I promise. He just...well, he felt as if he was telling you too much at once. He didn't want you to think he was lying."

"And I did think he was lying at first..."

"Colin only lies to protect his powers. Never for any other reason. He's a very honest man. All of my sons are."

"Do their wives know of their powers?"

Holli nodded. "Yes, all of them do. I'll have them all come over tomorrow afternoon and you can meet them."

"Will I like them?" Brynna asked, looking skeptical.

"Oh, yes. They are all very dear to me. Just as you are. You will have the hardest job of all, I must admit. Being the lady of the keep is not an easy task."

"I worry I won't know what to do. My mother...well, she rarely gave us lessons on running a household. Only my three eldest sisters learned how, and they are all married." Brynna looked down. "I believe they were going to make certain I never married. As the youngest, they just didn't care to give another dowry."

"Well, you'll marry now. It's hard to believe, but perhaps you being kidnapped was a good thing for your future."

Brynna laughed. "I can't imagine that could be true."

Holli looked skeptical. "Do you care to have a message sent to your parents that you are all right?"

"Nay. They have probably forgotten me by now. I've been gone a whole sennight, and they never really paid attention to me anyway. They may not even realize I'm gone."

"Oh, they know you're gone. No mother would not miss her daughter if she suddenly disappeared."

Brynna just smiled, not willing to argue. But her mother had never paid any attention to her. She and her sisters had shared a nurse, and only the nurse truly seemed to care. She really was fortunate to have been kidnapped, as crazy as that may seem. Well, now that her wounds were healed.

"What else must we do for the wedding?" Brynna asked, hoping Holli wouldn't ask anything else about her parents.

"We just really need to decide what to serve for the feast. Do you mind if the children come? Weddings tend to be the entire clan."

"Do they?" Brynna hadn't wanted a large wedding, but if that's how the clan did things, she would be just fine with it.

Holli nodded. "It will be loud and boisterous with many people milling about the keep. During the feast, all of mine and my husband's belongings will be taken to our cottage, and you will start your wedding without your husband's parents here." She pursed her lips. "Would you like me to find you a maid? I had one for many years, and I'd be happy to see to it that you have one. My nurse helped me and then she helped with our children. The boys come quickly. You'll deliver one, and it will seem as if you blink, and you are carrying the next."

"What if I can't bear sons?"

Holli laughed. "It won't matter if you can or not. You will. We have three healers in the family, and they will see that you deliver your sons safely. I have a feeling that your husband will be the one to take care of you."

"Do you think Colin and I are a good match?" Brynna couldn't stop worrying about how very different they were. Colin had been kind to her, but what if he was only kind until they married?

"I do think you're an excellent match. You haven't run screaming, and that is always a good thing. Colin cares for you already. He slept outside your room on the floor last night, worried about you waking in pain during the night. He has healed many people, but he's never slept outside their door."

Brynna smiled at that. "I like to think of him caring for me that way. I suppose we will be a good match after all. Even though I'm not from the future."

Holli laughed. "It does almost seem to be a prerequisite for marrying into the family, doesn't it?"

Chapter Four

Their supper that evening was truly an experience. Brynna was given a small portion of three entirely different meals and she tasted each as if they were the most important part of her day. "I think I want all three," she said, worried Holli would be upset if she chose so many.

Holli grinned. "Wonderful. I'll let Cook know after supper."

A moment later, a serving maid brought in plates full of a brown mixture. "Brownies?" Brynna asked.

Holli nodded. "Brownies are filled with chocolate, something else you wouldn't have had the opportunity to try yet."

As Brynna stared down at what looked like a brown cake, her stomach turned. The brownies that were supposed to be wonderful looked anything but. Tentatively, she used her spoon and took a small bite of the dessert. Her eyes grew wide, and she took a larger bite.

"I think we should have brownies. These are delicious!"

"Chocolate is a New World crop that you wouldn't have heard of yet," Holli said. "But it's a staple in my diet and those of my friends."

"I can understand why. I could eat this for every meal!"

Holli laughed. "We don't grow enough cocoa beans for that. We do enough for special events, and that's all. We don't dare introduce them to Europe before they're discovered."

Brynna sighed. "There's something wonderful about these brownies of yours."

Colin and his father watched the entire interaction, neither saying much of anything. Deciding what to have for the wedding feast was women's work after all.

After supper, they all retired to the parlor. Colin's parents sat on one sofa, and Colin and Brynna sat opposite them.

Colin had his arm loosely draped around Brynna's shoulders, and though she worried it might make his mother think less of her, Holli didn't seem bothered by it at all.

"Am I asking too much for all three of those delicious things to be served at my wedding feast?" Brynna asked, worried that she would cause too much work for the servants.

"Not at all!" Holli said. "It's what I serve for every feast. It satisfies us all."

"Well, then that sounds good to me." Brynna frowned. "I have no special dress to wear for the wedding. Will that matter?"

Holli's smile widened. "You'll wear a traditional McClain dress, of course. Like what I'm wearing."

"But I don't have..."

"You will," Holli promised. "I can't imagine Colin would marry you if you were dressed in anything else."

Colin laughed. "Mayhap not, but I would marry her if she was dressed in nothing..."

Brynna felt her face grow hot. She wanted to pull away from Colin, but his arm tightened around her. "'Tis not proper to say such things!"

Colin chuckled. "We're to have seven sons together, lass. No one will think any less of either of us if I desire you."

"But you should not say such things in front of your parents!"

He looked at his parents. "Does it surprise either one of you that I would like to see my affianced wife wearing nothing?"

When his parents both shook their heads, Brynna sighed. "I'm afraid my family was not so open about these things as you are."

"You were a family of daughters. If there had been sons, more would have been said about desiring another person."

"My only brother is two years younger than me and has already been promised in marriage. I think they are planning to let him do as he will for one more year, and then he will marry his chosen bride."

"Do you like the girl chosen for your brother?" Holli asked.

Brynna shrugged. "None of us have met her. My father met with her father to arrange all, but we were never given the choice of meeting her. They have been affianced for as long as I can remember."

Holli shook her head. "I know that's how things are done now, but in the future people marry for love."

Brynna sighed. "I always dreamed I'd marry for love. But it looks like I'm just another arranged marriage."

Colin looked at her, his eyes clouded. Without speaking aloud, he asked her in her head, "Would you prefer to wait until we have time to know one another better?"

"Would you be willing to wait?" she asked the same way.

"Nay. But I thought you would like to know that I care about your feelings."

She grinned at him, shaking her head.

Holli said then, "It's not fair when you use telepathy when talking to one another."

Colin looked at his mother with a grin. "Would you prefer we whispered in front of you? Or perhaps we excused ourselves, so I could go and kiss her as I've thought about nothing else through all this talk of wedding plans."

Holli sighed. "You know I'd prefer you participated in the conversation with all in the room and not just the one you've chosen."

They all heard the door of the keep slamming, and then a loud voice asked, "Father? Are you here?"

"That's my brother, Blake," Colin whispered to Brynna.

A man who looked much like Colin stepped into the parlor. "Father, there are rumors of an attack from the MacDonalds. 'Tis supposed to be here by seven days from now."

Colin looked at his father. Colin would be laird before the attack arrived, but he hoped his father would give whatever orders were necessary. When his father just looked back at him, Colin stood. "My wedding is two days hence. On the following day, we will ride to the south and meet their army."

Blake looked at Colin. "Aye, future laird." It was obvious Blake was trying hard not to laugh.

Colin nodded briefly, trying not to feed into his brother's amusement. If he was to be laird, he must show strength. "I will ride with you. Twill be nice to have two healers and two who can fling boulders with their minds."

"And two who can move at super speeds, and two who can communicate through minds. Aye, you are needed, Colin. I am to lead the men?"

"Aye. As always. My strength does not lie in my ability to wield a sword."

Blake shook his head. "Only because you refuse to train with us."

"Of course." Colin refused to train with the men daily. Once a week was more than enough for him to keep in shape and know his soldiers well. Besides, twas Blake's job to train the men. Not his.

Colin turned back to sit on the sofa with Brynna. "Brynna, this is my brother Blake. He's a year older than I am, but he acts as if he's a generation older."

Brynna nodded in deference. "It is good to meet you Blake."

"And you," Blake returned. He looked at the girl for a moment, realizing she had an English accent, but then he lowered his head in a bow. "I shall spread the word of the wedding and of riding out in three days."

With that, Blake left, and Brynna bit her lip. "You have to ride out the morning after our wedding?"

Colin grinned at her. "At least I won't miss the wedding night," he said with a lecherous look.

Holli laughed softly. "On that note, I think Bryson and I will excuse ourselves for a midnight stroll around the loch." She stood and Bryson followed suit, taking her hand. "Don't wait up!"

Brynna smiled as the older couple left the room, turning on her seat so she could face Colin more fully. "I like your mother a great deal. I always imagined, if I married, that I would be fighting my husband's mother all the time. That's how my older sisters make it seem."

"Oh, no one fights with my mother. She's been the lady of Clan McClain too long for that."

"I'm certain she has. I do enjoy being around her though. I enjoy our conversations, and your naked baby pictures..."

He laughed. "I promise, I've grown in many ways since that picture was taken."

Brynna blushed again, realizing exactly what he was talking about. "What will our wedding feast be like?" she asked. "Other than eating delicious food of course."

"You'll be introduced to the whole clan. There will be music and dancing. You'll meet all of my brothers' wives, who will become your new sisters. This family will have you just one sister less than you had," he told her.

She smiled. "I don't miss my father, but I do miss my sisters. We did everything together. I do hope I'll enjoy the sisters marriage to you will bring me."

"You will. I promise. They are all lovely lasses, and there are many nieces and nephews already. But none that will carry on the McClain tradition with the youngest son inheriting a power or the lairdship. That will be our sons."

"You don't think it odd that we're going into marriage knowing how many children we'll have and the gender of each?"

"I've always known. It's odd, I know, but for me it would be odd if it were different."

"I suppose that makes sense. Do any of the men in the family have seven daughters?"

He chuckled in response. "Not so far, but I wouldn't put it past my family. We tend to do things in odd ways all the time."

"I can see that." She smiled at him. "I do like your parents a great deal. I hope I'll like my new sisters just as much."

"I hope you like your future husband just as much. You keep talking about gaining new family members. Do you not want to gain a new husband?"

She blushed, looking down at her hands. "I think I'll be pleased to have you as husband."

He leaned toward her and kissed her, more passionately than he had before. He pulled her to him until she was sitting on his lap. "I know I'll be pleased with you as wife," he whispered, his hands roving over her body.

She gasped in shock. "You shouldn't touch me there!"

"Where?" he asked, his hands still moving.

"Colin!"

His lips found hers again, and her protests died in his kiss. When his hand cupped her breast, she was shocked, but at the same time, she enjoyed the touch.

It seemed like only a minute since his parents had left when they heard the door to the keep open. He held her where she was, not worried that his parents would find anything wrong with what they were doing. They were to be married in two days.

Bryson and Holli stopped at the door of the parlor and Bryson smiled. "Looks like you made good use of your time, son."

"I'm not the type to waste a minute, Dad."

Bryson laughed. "We'll leave you two alone and head to our bed. Get her to her room soon, and don't try to join her. You can wait two more days."

Colin sighed. "All right."

"Goodnight!" Holli called as they headed toward the stairs.

"I am so embarrassed," Brynna said, burying her face against his plaid. "I shouldn't have let you touch me that way. And your parents saw us!"

"My parents are happy that we care for one another. Dinna worry about what they saw."

She sighed. "Twill take a while for me to get used to a man touching me."

"Not too long I hope. And not just any man. Your husband."

"Aye. Just you, Colin. But not for two more days."

"You ask me to wait an eternity!" he complained.

She stood up. "I should sleep now. Tis getting late."

"Aye." He stood as well, taking her hand and leading her up the stairs. "Are you still sore anywhere? Do you need more healing?"

Remembering what it had felt like to have his hands on her legs the night before, she shook her head, trying not to let him see her blush. "I feel much better today."

"Good." At her door, he kissed her once more. "Dream of me, lass."

"Only if you promise to dream of me as well," she said boldly.

He laughed at that. "I will dream of how soft your flesh is, and how good you feel when I touch you."

She turned to her room, went inside, and closed the door behind her. Unfortunately, she could still hear his laugh with the door closed. He was the kind of man she'd always dreamed she'd marry. And it seemed to be happening very quickly. And her heart was weakening toward him. How on earth could she fall in love with a man who would have absolute power over her?

Nay, she refused to love him until she knew how he would treat her after they married.

As she lay in bed, she couldn't help but think about him and how it felt with his hands on her body. Perhaps her wedding night wasn't something to be feared after all. Maybe it was something for her to look forward to. He was a good man after all.

By the morning of her wedding, Brynna was just a ball of nerves. Colin wasn't helping at all when he pulled her into a corner every time she saw him and kissed her until her knees were weak. She had no idea where her head was most of the time.

Soon after she woke, a tub was carried into the room, followed by a row of servants with buckets of hot water. As soon as they were gone, she removed her nightgown and sank into the hot water.

She quickly washed herself and even washed her hair, wanting to look her very best for Colin on their wedding day. She was just finishing in the tub, and was drying off with a cloth she'd been given for that purpose when a knock came at the door.

"It's just me, Brynna," came Holli's voice.

"Come in then!" Brynna stood with the drying cloth in front of her, and she smiled when she saw the brush Holli was carrying.

"I had thought to have a maid trained for Colin's wife before he married, but the two of you surprised me with how quickly things are moving."

Brynna took the chair Holli pointed to with the brush, and sat, letting the older woman brush her hair dry. "I will get your wedding dress in a moment. I thought you might enjoy wearing some pearls with it, some I brought from the future."

"Oh, I'd enjoy that a great deal!" Brynna said. "Thank you for treating me as if I'm your own daughter on her wedding day."

"Oh, you have no idea how excited I am that Colin has finally found a bride. I love all my sons, and all of my grandchildren, but Colin's sons will be special to our clan. They will be our leaders."

Brynna sighed. "And I will bear them all."

Holli laughed. "I did it, and so can you."

"I shall remember you said that."

Chapter Five

Her wedding day was little more than a blur for Brynna. The actual wedding was over quickly, but the feast that followed was not. She met each of Colin's brothers, and his brothers' wives, and then she was introduced one at a time to those in the clan.

It was all just a whirl. She vaguely remembered eating the feast later, and Colin being patted on the back repeatedly. She danced with Colin, his brothers, and his father.

At the end of the day, when the keep was empty but for those who lived there, Brynna was surprised to see his parents head for the door. "Where are you going?"

"We told you we'd move out when you married," Holli said, smiling. "It's your turn to lead the clan, and our turn to enjoy retirement."

"I didn't think you'd go today! Can't you at least wait for a few more days?" Brynna wasn't worried about that night, but she didn't like the idea of being home alone while her husband was off dealing with a battle with another clan.

Holli seemed to understand. Taking Brynna's hands in hers, she said, "I'll stay with you while Colin is off. Would that make you feel better?"

Brynna nodded emphatically. After all the hours she'd spent blindfolded and alone, the idea of having to stay in the keep by herself was frightening. "It would make me feel much better. Thank you."

Holli kissed her cheek. "You're my daughter now. Ask me for what you need."

"She needs no one tonight but her husband," Colin said. "We'll leave at noon to meet the MacDonalds. But for now, I'm insisting on my wedding night."

Holli laughed. "Enjoy yourselves."

As his parents left the keep, Brynna turned to Colin. "Mayhap we could postpone the wedding night for a week or two? When you get back is soon enough, isn't it?"

Colin slowly shook his head. "Five minutes from now isn't soon enough." He swept her up in his arms and carried her to the top of the stairs. She expected him to take her to the room she'd used for the past few nights, but instead, he turned left at the top of the stairs and carried her into the bedroom that had belonged to his parents.

"We're not going to my room?" she asked as he set her on her feet in the bedchamber.

Colin slowly shook his head. "Of course not, lass. This is our room now." His hands immediately went to the top of her dress and the brooch that kept her tartan up.

She batted his hands away. "We could talk for a little while first," she implored.

He shook his head. "You're going to be nervous until this first time is over. No need for that."

This time when his hands went to the brooch, she didn't protest, and he carefully unwrapped her tartan, letting it fall at her feet. And when she stood in front of him in just her blouse, he lowered his head and kissed her. All of his hands—what seemed like at least twenty of them—roamed her body, and she felt his touch on her bare legs, cupping her breast through her blouse, and under her blouse moving over her bare back.

She didn't know how it happened, but soon she was bare, and he was lowering her onto the bed. Watching while he undressed, she knew she should look away, but his body looked like something made of clay by the finest sculptor.

His eyes met hers as the last bit of his clothing touched the floor. She was excited for his lovemaking after the kissing and touching they'd done, but she lay abed watching him. There was a tiny bit of fear mixed with a whole lot of excitement running through her veins, and she couldn't wait until he joined her.

When his weight came down on the bed, she felt the shift, but she opened her arms for him. She wanted to touch him the way he'd touched her. First, her fingers moved over his face, prickly with the day's growth of beard.

She didn't much remember what happened after that, as he immediately suckled her nipple into his mouth as his hands went to the juncture of her thighs.

When he entered her, she felt the second of pain she'd expected, but then it only felt good to her. It was glorious to have him atop her and inside her as he drove them both toward something—she didn't know what—but something wonderful.

Later, as she lay in his arms with her head pillowed atop his shoulder, she asked, "Is it always like that between a man and a woman?"

"If the two care for one another, yes," he said, still a bit out of breath.

"Then I shall look forward to your return home." She went up on one elbow and looked down into his face. She'd promised herself she wouldn't love him until she knew he was a truly good man, but...as he lay there with his hair tousled, and a wicked gleam in his eye, she fell the rest of the way in love, as if she was rolling down a great hill. "I will happily do that again and again."

He grinned at her, cupping the back of her neck and pulling her down for a kiss. "You are the woman I've waited my entire life for. I could feel it as soon as you suggested that I be your husband. It felt right."

She sighed contentedly, resting half beside him and half atop him. "I don't know how my sisters ever complained about having to do that with their husbands. They acted as if it was something to be dreaded, and to me...well, it's something to be enjoyed."

"God made us with the ability to do this. We should all be grateful for his love."

"And I'm so thankful He did."

BRYNNA WOKE EARLY THE next morning, falling back to the way she'd always done things in England before she was abducted. Colin was still sleeping soundly, so she rose quietly, dressing quickly, and she headed down the stairs to the kitchen. Once there, she smiled at the Cook. "Is it possible for me to get breakfast?"

Cook turned to her and smiled. "As the mistress of the keep, anything you request, we will do."

Brynna smiled. "I thank you."

"Porridge? Or something heartier?" the cook asked.

"Porridge sounds like the perfect way to begin my day."

"I agree." Cook hurried to scoop some porridge out of the pot in front of her. "It's what I had this morning as well."

Brynna smiled, accepting the bowl. She carried it into the great hall to sit at the table for her meal. She ate in silence, thinking about how much her husband had come to mean to her in such a short time.

Just before she finished, he appeared before her. "Porridge?" he asked.

She nodded. "It's delicious."

"Then I shall get myself a bowl." He hurried to the kitchen and Cook followed him out with his bowl of porridge a moment later.

To her surprise, Colin sat beside her at the table, instead of at one end. It was nice to have breakfast only with him.

"You plan on leaving around noon?" she asked.

Colin nodded. "Aye, that's the plan. I will not lead the men, as I never do, but I will bring up the rear and help with my powers. I do not train often with my men. Tis not something I enjoy or really need to do with my abilities."

"How do your abilities help in a war?" she asked.

"I will sometimes pick up one of the enemies and fling him at the crowd with my mind. I can move quickly enough that I can move one of our men, and replace him with one of the enemy, so that the enemy is fighting it's own people. Things like that. I do carry a sword and use it if necessary, but I would rather use my powers. They are more creative."

"Have you been in many battles?" Brynna asked, hoping he wouldn't see many in the future.

"I have not. Only five or six. I must go this time as the laird. My men will be bolstered by my presence on the field."

"I do hope you'll be careful. There are sons to beget."

He chuckled. "I will be fine. I not only have powers on my side, but I also have the luck that comes with being the seventh son of a seventh son."

She nodded, not quite convinced he'd be all right, but it did seem as if his powers would carry him through. "I hope you'll still take care."

He nodded. "I will. I need to get home to my bride!"

"Will your father go?"

"He will. He won't fight, but he'll be there. This will be his last battle."

"I'm glad I'll have your mother with me. I know I can't ask it of her every time you leave the village, but hopefully there will always be someone I can ask."

"Any of my brothers' wives would come stay with you as well. They'd love the time away from cooking."

Brynna smiled. "I had not thought of that. I can see where it would be like taking a holiday to spend time here in the keep."

He nodded. "I do believe that's how they'd all see it. My mother always had grandmother and Aunt Alyssa, and even Great Grandmother come stay. The four of them are all from the future, and truly enjoy one another's company."

"I still have a hard time believing they are all from the future."

"You saw my mother's phone. She showed you naked baby pictures on it."

"'Tis true. Still, it sounds very far-fetched."

Colin shrugged. "I guess growing up knowing your mother came from the future and your family has magical powers is different than meeting a family where those things have happened. I never doubted it."

Brynna smiled. "Mayhap you are more gullible than me."

He laughed at that. "I do not believe that's what it is."

"What do I need to prepare for you to take on this trip?" she asked, changing the subject.

He frowned for a moment. "There is nothing. Cook will gather food for me, and I will sleep under the tartan I wear."

"I could send something else for you to sleep under."

"There is no need. We Scots are from hardy stock. Sleeping under a tartan is perfect. We have no need to bring tents and servants along to a battle. We prefer to be more self-sufficient than that."

"There is nothing I can do to ready you for your trip?" Brynna wasn't certain if she was relieved or feeling useless. She wanted to help him.

He shook his head. "Nay. Not a thing. I've done this many times before with no help from a wife."

"That is sad," she said. "You should always have help from a wife." Especially one who loves you as much as I do.

"I shall be fine. The food Cook is preparing is all that is needed for the journey. She prepares enough for the entire army, and we all share.

She makes the journey much easier. All of the food is dried oatcakes or dried beef. No one is needed to cook."

"You won't get tired of eating those foods?"

"We won't be gone long enough to tire of them. This should take four days at most."

"Four days?" It sounded like forever to Brynna.

"Aye. Aren't you glad we won't be attacking England?" He grinned at her. "That would take a great deal longer."

She grinned. "Well, I suppose I'd rather not see you fighting with my father and his men."

"Does your father command a strong army?"

Brynna shrugged. "I really do not know. I've never seen an army other than his, and his men rarely fight. Father doesn't even train them any longer. He lets someone else do the work."

"All right. Hopefully my army will never be required to test your father's army's mettle."

She stood on tiptoe, kissed him quickly and held him tight. "I shall never forgive you if you die during this battle."

He laughed. "I'll bear that in mind."

His mother came to the door then with a strange-looking bag. It was obviously filled with what they'd need for the days the men would be gone. Brynna was surprised to see Holli was followed by the wives of Colin's brothers. "I thought we'd make a party of it."

Brynna bit her lip. "I have no feast prepared for a party."

"Oh, I'll let the cook know that we're all here, and she'll make it work for us. She's wonderful like that." Holli disappeared into the kitchen and came back with a smile. Looking at Colin, she said, "The men are about to leave. Have fun and we will try not to miss you all."

There were over a dozen small children who looked around them as if they were truly at a place for a magical party. Brynna couldn't help but smile. "Shall we go in the parlor?"

The sisters smiled. "We'll each put our things in the room our husband had as a child first. Even Mother can put her things in the room Father used as a child, because he was also the seventh son." Brynna couldn't remember the name of the sister who spoke, but she knew it was the wife of Colin's eldest brother. Hopefully she'd know all their names before the weekend was over.

While Brynna watched with a bemused look on her face, all of her new sisters and Holli ran up the stairs. The children gathered around her. "Did you really marry Uncle Colin?" one little girl with bright red hair asked.

Brynna smiled. "I did marry your uncle."

"And now you get to have seven sons," a little boy said.

"That I do. Do you think I'll be good at having seven sons?"

The boy shook his head. "No one is a better mother than mine, so I don't think so."

"Maybe your mother could give me lessons on how to be the best mother in the world."

The boy cocked his head to one side. "Mayhap, but you can't be better than her. Maybe you can be the second best mother."

"That would still be good though, right?"

The boy shrugged. You wouldn't be the best though..."

The women started down the stairs, and Brynna whispered, "Which one is your mother?"

"The prettiest of them all!"

The little red haired girl frowned. "No, my mother is the prettiest."

"Now you're lying. I'm telling your mother!"

Brynna couldn't help laughing as the women joined her and the children. She could tell she was going to have such a wonderful time she wouldn't miss Colin at all.

Chapter Six

Brynna couldn't honestly say she didn't miss Colin, but with all of her guests, she didn't miss him as much as she'd thought she would. The women stayed up late each night, and while the children slept, Brynna learned to read.

It wasn't at all difficult as she'd been told. Why, she took to it like a fish to water, and by the time the men returned she could read one of the books Holli had brought from the future. She wasn't a fast reader, but she understood what the letters meant on the page, and it was a gift that she would always cherish.

The men got home on the evening of the fourth day, and Brynna rushed to the door when she heard Colin, throwing herself into his arms. "Was the battle bad? Are you all right?"

Colin laughed. "The battle didn't happen. I was able to talk with the leader of the MacDonalds, and we came to an agreement. They will trade us some of their oats and wheat, and we will provide healing help whenever it's needed. They were coming here just to ask me for healing help for some of their soldiers who had been maimed. I healed some and Archie healed some with our healing potions, and they were satisfied with that. They are sending ten cows in payment."

"How badly were they maimed?"

"I grew a leg onto one of the soldiers. I acted like I was shocked my healing potion worked so well, and that made it all right with the men. I think they would have accepted anything we said as long as they had the results they wanted."

Brynna covered her mouth when a giggle threatened to pop out. She could just picture the surprise on the men's faces as a leg grew from where a stump had been. "I wish I could have seen that. Not the growing of the leg, but the look on all the men's faces."

Colin grinned. "I guess I never thought of it that way. I always worry about covering my secret, not thinking about how funny it must be to see the people's shock. You help me look at the world in a whole new way."

Brynna had walked away from the women and children upon hearing Colin's arrival. She heard a commotion behind her and turned, seeing that all the women and children were packed and ready to go back to their own homes. "Thank you all for coming and making the time go by faster! And for teaching me to read!"

Holli hugged her. "You'll be fine now that Colin is home, so we'll be on our way. And you are a fantastic reader. I'm waiting for you to start writing your own stories."

"I don't think that is coming anytime soon." Brynna already found herself shortening words the same way Colin and his family did.

As she said goodbye to all of her new sisters and nieces and nephews, Brynna realized she would miss them not being with her every day. Mayhap she could find a reason for them to all gather once or twice a week. It would bring her more joy than she could express.

Just as seeing Colin brought her joy, but she also felt a stirring in a place a lady just didn't mention having. She was ready to go upstairs and enjoy her husband again. "Are you hungry?" she asked.

Colin nodded. "Famished. I can only eat the food we take with us for a short time."

"We had soup made of potatoes tonight. I'll fetch some from the kitchen."

Colin sat at the table, slumping a little. He had pushed the men hard to get them back so quickly, but he couldn't figure out why he'd be married if he couldn't enjoy his wife.

When she returned with a large bowl of soup, and some brown bread, he smiled. "Thank you, wife."

"It seems so odd that someone would call me that." She sat across from him at the table. "I never thought I'd be able to marry."

He took a bite before answering. "I can't imagine a woman as pretty as you wouldn't marry. Your parents should have been looking for a husband for you years ago."

Brynna shrugged. "I always knew a marriage would be unlikely for me. Though I'm not pleased I was kidnapped, I'm happy that you found me and were willing to marry me."

He reached out and squeezed her hand. "I couldn't have done anything else."

When he'd finished his meal, she took his bowl and the plate she'd brought the bread on and carried both into the kitchen, putting them on the work table there. Cook was still there and smiled at her as she took the dishes and dropped them in her basin of steaming water.

"We'd like porridge for breakfast in the morning, if you don't mind, Cook."

"I am happy to make it." Cook smiled at Brynna. "I'm going to enjoy having you be the lady of our clan."

Brynna smiled. "I'm happy we're working together."

When she got to the dining room, it was empty. She had no idea where Colin had gone. But as she looked for him, she heard in her head. "I'm upstairs waiting for you."

Laughing, she shook her head and headed to the stairs. When she got to the bedchamber she shared with Colin, he was sitting on the edge of the bed. "Are you all right?"

Colin nodded. "Tired but all right. Twas a long journey and there was much healing to be done. I pray that I'll sleep for a week."

She laughed. "Would rubbing your shoulders help?"

Colin shook his head. "I'll have my mother do it tomorrow. She was something called a massage therapist before she came back in time, and she works my muscles like no one else."

Brynna frowned. If he'd rather have his mother work on his muscles, then she could just do it. "All right. What can I do for you then?"

He looked at her with his eyes half closed. "I'd drag you to bed with me if I had the energy to do it. Instead I'll invite you to bed so I can hold you all night. Lovemaking will have to wait until I've had some sleep."

She thought it was odd that he was too tired to make love with her, but if that was the case, then she would simply wait until he wasn't too tired. It felt odd to disrobe in front of him, knowing nothing would happen between them, but she decided not to worry too much about it as she shed her clothes, and climbed into bed beside him.

Colin didn't bother to take off his shirt, he simply threw his kilt to the floor and settled beside her, pulling her to him so that he could hold her close. "Did you miss me?" he asked softly.

"I had a house party while you were gone. How could I have had time to miss you?" Even as the words came out, she called herself a liar. But what good would it do for him to realize she already loved him? It would give him too much power over her, and that was that.

"Well, I missed you," he whispered as his eyes drifted closed. He was too tired to think about what she'd said or anything else. Sleep was all he cared about.

BY THE TIME COLIN WOKE the following morning, Brynna was long gone. He put his hand on the spot where she'd laid, and it was cool to the touch. He'd hoped for a nice rousing round of newlywed fun, but apparently, she'd had other things on her agenda that day.

The sun was high in the sky when he went downstairs to eat his breakfast. He was usually awake before the sun was up, but the trip had been exhausting. Not many understood how drained it made him to use his powers. And his powers had been used a great deal, as well as his brother's. He was just glad he'd been able to sit his horse on the way home, and hadn't had to ride face down, thrown over the saddle.

He found Brynna in the parlor with a book in her hands. "Have you broken your fast?"

Brynna nodded. "I have. Would you like me to sit with you while you eat?"

"Aye. That would please me a great deal." He took her hand and they walked into the great hall together, and went to the dining area.

"I'll ask Cook for your food." Brynna went into the kitchen and brought back a bowl of porridge. "I made sure Cook knew to save some of the porridge for you. I was worried it would be gone before you woke."

"Thank you," he accepted the bowl and covered her hand with his as she sat opposite him. "This is exactly what I need in the morning. A good bowl of porridge and a beautiful wife to gaze upon."

Brynna blushed at his words. "Do you have plans for the day?"

He shook his head. "I made certain all the men knew that I was taking today to spend with my bride. I have no desire to deal with anything about the clan. They know what's important enough to come to me with, and it's someone losing a limb or dying. And for those things they can go to my brother."

"Oh my!" She couldn't help but be flattered that he wanted to spend time with her so badly. "So what shall we do today?"

"I want to show you the whole area. I want to walk with you through the woods and show you all the places I played as a child. I wish you could return the favor, but I don't believe that's wise."

Brynna shook her head. "My parents have probably forgotten all about me already."

"I'm the youngest of seven sons, and I never felt forgotten."

"Because in your family, the youngest is the most important. It's not the same with most families. In our case, only the son, the ninth child was important."

He shook his head. "I hope you know that I will think of all of our boys as important. I don't think it's right for anyone to favor one child over another."

She smiled. "I feel exactly the same. I do wish I could explain to my parents how I felt being last in their eyes, but I don't think it would do any good. They already had their favorite grandchildren, after all."

"Your speech is becoming a great deal more futuristic."

"It's your mother's books. I can't stop reading, and their speech patterns are so different than ours."

"Aye. I can understand that. I'm glad you had people to keep you occupied while I was away. Now they all need to go away, so I can have my wife to myself."

She laughed. "I don't think that will be a problem. They're all happy to have their husbands home."

"I'm sure that's true." He finished his porridge and stood. "Let's go for that walk."

"Let me take your bowl to the kitchen first."

Colin frowned. "You're not a servant."

"I know I'm not. But I do have a moment to take a bowl to the kitchen so Cook doesn't need to come out and search for it." Brynna was certain that part of being happy was having a good relationship with the people who served in the keep. She was back a moment later. "We're having a beef roast for supper, and more of those potatoes. I hope your clan grows a great deal of them."

He chuckled. "We do. And more than that, they are only served at the keep. No one else gets them."

"Oh, good. I find I like them too much to want to share."

Taking her hand, he led her out of the keep into the sunlight. She'd spent every afternoon while he was gone outside beside the loch, and the other wives and all the children had sat in the grass and enjoyed themselves. Holli had called it a picnic, and others from the clan had joined them. It had been great fun, but she'd always wished Colin was there beside her.

"Did you spend any time at the loch while I was gone?" he asked.

"We had what your mother called picnics there every day. We'd spread a blanket on the grass and we'd eat our midday meal while the children frolicked and played. Twas great fun."

He smiled. "We'll have a picnic of our own beside the loch soon. Maybe tomorrow."

"Won't you have clan business to tend to tomorrow?"

Colin sighed. "I'm used to having most of my days free. Father would teach me how to run the clan in the morning, and I'd wander off and do whatever I wanted in the afternoons. I see now why my brothers thought I was a wastrel."

"A wastrel?" She tried the word and found she liked it. "Like a lazy man who does nothing all day long?"

"Exactly," he said. "Just like that."

"You're not a wastrel. You found me during one of your walks, and you healed me, and brought me home with you." She stopped walking and looked at him, her head tilted to one side. "Did you think you would end up married to me when you met me that day?"

He chuckled. "You were covered in mud and tied to a tree. I wasn't sure what to do with you at first."

She smiled. "If I had been hideously ugly under all that dirt, would you have agreed to marry me?"

"I guess we'll never know because you weren't hideously ugly under the dirt. You emerged from the dirt as a beautiful lass, one I could never reject." He put his hands on her waist and drew her to him, kissing her passionately. He wanted to carry her up to their bedchamber, but he had the feeling she wouldn't be happy with him being so bold about it.

He broke off the kiss when he heard cheers. "That's the way to kiss her, Laird!"

He looked over to see the family of the stablemaster watching them. The wife elbowed her husband in the ribs. "Leave the laird and his lady alone. They're newlyweds."

"Aye. They are." The family turned away and looked for a place for the picnic lunch they'd brought to the loch.

Colin wrapped his arm around her shoulders. "I want to show you around, but I also want to make love with ye, lass."

"We can go to our room for now and finish our walk later."

"Great idea, lass."

He picked her up in his arms, and it felt like he took two steps to be back at the front of the keep. "I'll race you upstairs!"

"No fair cheating!"

Chapter Seven

Colin and Brynna didn't make it out of their bedchamber until much later in the day. "I thought we were going to finish our walk," Brynna said looking toward the window and seeing it was getting dark.

"I guess I forgot my intentions," he said as he nibbled at one of her fingers.

"We can't spend all our time abed! We need to go out and spend time with the clan."

He laughed. "Forget the clan. I'm making love with my wife!"

She giggled. "I think the clan would miss us, and I have a feeling your parents would take turns thrashing us."

He frowned. "Did your parents thrash you?"

"Don't all parents?"

He shook his head, an angry look on his face. "My parents didn't. They talked to us about what we did wrong. Took away our ability to play outside. But they never hit us. Not once."

"My father thrashed us for the littlest things. I was outside when I was supposed to be working on my needlepoint, so my father used his belt. The side with the buckle. I hated when he did that."

Colin dropped her fingers and sat up in bed. "He hit you with the metal of his belt buckle?"

She nodded. "That was the worst thrashing. My brother was never punished. He could do no wrong in father's eyes. I could do no right. And he'd call me by all of my sisters names before he finally remembered mine."

"Mayhap we'll need to take a little trip to England and have a talk with your father. He needs to know you're safe anyway."

She laughed. "I'm sure they never noticed there was one less daughter. They simply didn't care about me. And that's fine."

"It is not fine. They will not be allowed to be around our sons. Not if they are going to treat them as they treated you!"

She didn't understand why he was so upset about the thrashings she'd received. She'd assumed every parent thrashed their child, just as every man beat his wife when she did something wrong. "I don't know why this angers you."

"Because you didn't deserve to be treated that way. Did you deliberately get into mischief?"

"Never! I never would." Brynna shook her head adamantly. "I tried to be invisible and quiet and not get noticed."

"I'm sure you did." He shook his head, the perplexed look still on his face. Did she not understand she deserved to be treated with love at all times? He wanted to lay siege to her parents' home.

"It's past time for supper," Brynna said. "Shall we go down?" She was looking forward to the roast beef and what the cook had called mashed potatoes. She'd loved all the potatoes she'd tried so far.

Colin dressed mumbling under his breath, and Brynna watched him for a moment before putting on her own clothing. He was very upset over what she'd told him, but she sensed he wasn't angry with her, but with her parents.

"Did your mother ever thrash you?"

She started to shake her head. "Once. But father told her if she didn't thrash me she would be thrashed, and she was recovering from him using his belt on her bare back, so she really had no choice. And little strength to thrash me as he would have liked."

Colin took a deep breath, walking to her, and tipping her chin up with one finger. "No wonder you didn't seem bothered by the fact you were treated poorly by your abductors. You expect to be treated that way. I tell you now, if anyone ever raises a hand to you again, I will thrash them myself."

She wrapped her arms around him and just held him, feeling very protected when his arms came around her. She knew it would be different when he became angry with something she did, but it was nice to hear that he never planned to hurt her.

They went down for supper, and Cook served them with a big grin on her face. "I thought you were to spend the day walking, but instead you spent it in bed. We'll have the oldest of those seven sons here in no time." She put mashed potatoes, roast beef, carrots, and bread on the table. "Would you like wine with your meal?"

At Colin's nod, Brynna smiled. "It will be my first sip of wine."

"You've never had wine?" he asked. "I've had it with special meals since I was a boy."

"And this is a special meal?" she asked, surprised.

"It's my first supper with just my wife since we married. Aye, it's a special meal."

Brynna smiled and reached out to take Colin's hand. "You make me feel like I'm special and not just Brynna, the girl who was always in the way."

"You are special. And you will be treated as such by everyone around you."

She laughed softly. "It sounds wonderful, but I'm not certain you can make it happen."

"Trust me," he said, filling his plate with the food in front of them. "You're going to love mashed potatoes. Especially with the gravy Cook serves with it. Truly, this is my favorite meal, but don't tell my mother. She thinks I should like her Irish nachos best. But as far as I know, Ireland has never seen a potato, just as we hadn't."

She shrugged. "I know nothing but that I like the taste of these potatoes."

He reached across the table and added just a touch of gravy to her potatoes. "Now try it."

She took another bite of her potatoes, and her eyes opened. "That's delicious! I want gravy with every meal then!"

He laughed. "I told Cook when I was a boy that she would have to serve gravy with every meal when I was laird."

"And so far, she's doing it!"

He nodded. "It sure is good to be laird!"

COLIN WAS SINGING A different tune when all of his responsibilities crashed down on him the following day. His father came to report another clan was on their way. "Can the men go without me this time?" Colin asked. "I have spent two nights with my new wife."

"I heard you spent all day in bed with her yesterday, son. Not sure what you're complaining about."

Colin sighed. "Do we know why they're coming?"

"They've just come back from warring with the English. My guess is they want healing. Our clan has been known to heal everyone for generations."

"How far from us?"

"They're on Campbell land now."

"So they're very close. I guess we ride to Campbell land."

"I suppose we must."

"I'll go and have the stablemaster saddle the horses." Colin wasn't looking forward to the ride to his cousins' land, but he would go.

"I'll let the stablemaster and the men know we're riding out. Let your bride know what you're doing. She seems to be a worrier."

"Someday, I'll know what kind of woman she is. I wish I could wait a month before I had to take over as laird. My wife will be a stranger when our third son is born."

His father laughed and clapped him on the back. "Tis not an easy life, but it's a good one."

Colin went to find Brynna in the parlor where she was reading yet another of his mother's books. He was a bit worried that she was spending too much time with books and not enough taking care of the keep, but he could tell that everything was perfectly clean.

"Lass, I need to ride out to my cousin's land, near where I found you. There is another army coming our way, but we believe they come for healing only, and maybe for a peace treaty."

Brynna sighed. "Will ye be home for supper?"

"I should be. It's a short ride. It depends on how many men need to be healed."

She stood and kissed him. "Safe trip, Colin. I'll be waiting for you to return."

Colin met his mother on the way out of the keep. "She's in the parlor," he said automatically, knowing his mother wasn't there to check on him. Nay, she was there to support his new wife.

Many of the soldiers were headed to the stable, with a few already atop their horses. Colin had seldom ridden with the men when they were off to meet another army. Nay, he'd stayed at home where it was safe.

His horse was already saddled, and he quickly mounted. "The goal is to be home for supper!" He called out to the men.

There was a roar of laughter, but the men raised their right arms and yelled, "Home for supper!"

Colin looked for his brother Archie in the crowd and moved his horse toward him. "Father thinks this is another healing mission. Why don't they just send word that a healer is needed?"

Archie shook his head. "I suppose we'll be needed more than anyone else this evening."

"I guess so." Colin wanted just a week straight home with his wife. By that time the newness of marriage would be over, and he could forget her.

As they rode toward Campbell land, Colin thought of his beautiful wife at home with only his mother and a book to keep her company. He was certain she'd be happy.

THE MEN WERE HOME FOR supper that night, having made an agreement with the laird of Clan Cameron. The clan would send for a healer when they needed one without sending their entire army. Colin was satisfied with the results of the day.

When he walked into the keep, exhausted as he had just two days before, his wife was there to greet him with a kiss. "All went well?"

He nodded. "Aye. They needed healing after their war with the English, but the next time they need healing, they will send a messenger and not an entire army. I asked them to spread the word that the McClains would heal those who are sick or injured, even if they are enemies. They simply have to send word."

"Your great-grandfather made the same deal with the clans when he was laird." Holli smiled at her son. "I must go feed my husband."

Cook walked out of the kitchen then. "You will not. Bring the former laird here. I made enough for all."

"Thank you, Cook," Holli said. "I will go fetch Bryson then."

As soon as Cook was back in the kitchen, Colin said, "Father is coming. No need to fetch him."

Holli laughed. "I love that power of yours. But I do wish you'd let us know how everything goes after you meet with the other clan. There's no reason not to, is there?"

"I suppose we could. I've never tried over a great distance, but I will see if it works the next time I'm called away by my duties."

Brynna enjoyed eating with his parents. Holli and Bryson regaled Brynna with stories about mischief the boys had gotten into. "We expected seven sons of course, but we didn't expect seven powerful sons. We thought only the youngest would have powers, but it didn't work out that way for us."

"I see that!" Brynna said, smiling. "It must have been strange to discover each boy had a power."

"Very strange," Holli agreed. "Colin had the powers of all of his brothers from the time he could walk, but they made a pact not to tell Bryson and me. They thought it was a fun secret. I was so relieved when I found out Colin had powers!"

"I can understand that! I think I would have been relieved as well."

"Just wait until you have mischievous sons. They will make you crazy even as you gaze upon them with all the love in your heart." Holli shook her head. "Colin was always wandering off, and I would think he'd never come back, but he was always here for supper."

Bryson grinned. "His rally cry as we left the village today was, 'Home for supper!' The men laughed, but they sure echoed him."

Colin grinned sheepishly. "I like food. And my beautiful wife asked me if I'd be home for supper."

After supper Colin's parents went home, and Colin and Brynna spent some time in the parlor. Brynna worked on needlepoint while she and Colin talked. "Have I ever mentioned how much I hate needlepoint?" she asked.

He shook his head. "No?"

"Well, I do. It's what young ladies are supposed to do, but I always end up with a bloodstained pattern because I stab myself with the needles I'm working with. Truly I don't know why I do it other than I'm supposed to!"

"You're not required to do any more needlepoint," Colin said.

"I'm not? Ever?"

He laughed. "Not if you don't enjoy it and it makes you bleed."

She looked at the design in her hands and flung it across the room. "I will never do it again then."

He chuckled. "Now that you're not holding anything sharp, you should move closer to me."

She giggled as she moved to sit much closer to her husband. "I'd rather sit close to you than do needlepoint any day."

"But you don't like needlepoint, so I don't feel like you're giving me a great compliment."

"Well, I am. You should be pleased with it!"

"Is that so?"

She snuggled closer to him and touched her tongue to his neck, wondering what his skin would taste like. He'd certainly licked hers more than once. It was salty, but she had no real occasion to keep tasting. He got to his feet and pulled her to the stairs with him. At the bottom, he picked her up and teleported to the top of the stairs.

"That was scary!" she said.

Colin ignored her comment as he carried her into their room and tossed her onto the bed. In seconds he was naked and he joined her, much to her delight.

He stripped her as quickly as he had himself and in moments they were locked together in love. She had no idea what she'd done to deserve a man like Colin, but when she found out what it was, she was certain to do it again and again.

The man made her heart pound faster even as he made her feel unfathomable joy. She'd fallen in love much too quickly, but she couldn't go back. He was hers forever, even if she had to bear seven sons with no hope of daughters. Granddaughters and nieces would make her happy.

No, her seventh son had to be the best seventh son who had ever lived.

Chapter Eight

Within a few days, word had gone out to all the Highland clans that if they simply asked for healing, someone would be sent to help them. A messenger came to them just a week later, asking for a healer to go to Clan MacPherson.

The MacPhersons had been an enemy of the McClains for generations, but Colin knew he had to go. Archie needed to stay with his wife, who was due to give birth any day, and he would be the clan's healer while Colin was gone.

While the messenger waited, Colin discussed the need to go with his father. "Do you think I'll be safe without a small contingent of armed men?"

Father immediately shook his head. "There is no chance you could be safe. Tis a long journey, and you will need at least ten men going with you."

Colin sighed. "I was hoping I could take Brynna with me this time, but in a camp with eleven men is no place for a gently bred lady like herself."

"I don't know about that, Colin. She's a strong lass, or she would have lost her mind after the kidnapping. I think she could do it without a problem."

"Really?" Colin grew excited. Yes, the journey would be long, and it would be hard, but at least they'd be together. "I'll ask her if she'd like to accompany me." Instead of getting up, he explained the situation and his proposal for her to come in his head. He smiled when he heard her shout yes back to him.

"She's going. Which men should I take?" Colin asked.

"Ask your brother. I'm no longer laird, remember?" Father had a pleased look on his face as he said the words. He was truly happy with his retirement.

Less than an hour later, they left the village with the MacPherson messenger. "Who is ill?" Colin asked. The man said nothing.

Colin frowned. If he wouldn't say, it must be the laird. And it was Colin's duty to keep him alive. If the man died, it would be war between the clans, and by the time all their allies were called upon, the war would stretch across the Highlands. No, he knew there must be peace, which meant healing the leader of his enemies. But he would keep his word and do as he was asked.

Twas a six-night journey to the keep of Clan MacPherson, and Colin and Brynna were able to sneak off for some private time every night. "I'm happy this happened in the summer," Colin said. "I wouldn't like the idea of you out in the cold."

"I'm fine," Brynna said, shaking her head. "I'm not made of glass." As soon as the words were out of her mouth, Brynna put her hand to her stomach. "I fear supper is not agreeing with me."

Colin's eyes widened. "I have oatcakes. They should calm your system."

Brynna turned and ran from Colin. Just the mention of food made her lose everything she'd had in her stomach all day.

Colin stood waiting for her to come back to him. Instead, he found her sitting on the bank of a small stream they were camped near. She was hugging her legs to her chest, crying.

He walked to her and sat down beside her, a suspicion growing in his mind. "Are you all right now?" he asked, looking at her closely.

"I just don't feel well. I shouldn't have come along with you." She felt as if her illness would make the entire trip more difficult for the men. This was only the second day of travel, and they had many to go.

"Have you forgotten I'm a healer?" he asked softly.

Her eyes widened. "I think of you as a healer for injuries, not for sickness."

"I have a feeling you're not sick."

"Do you think I pretended to vomit? I assure you, it's not something I would do!"

He smiled, reaching out to put his hand on her knee. He closed his eyes and concentrated on what was ailing his wife, and then he knew. "You're expecting."

"It's too soon!"

"It's not. I sometimes think that a McClain man could marry, wait a week, and his wife would be pregnant regardless of whether he made love with her."

"But...shouldn't I be vomiting later? Certainly not now!"

"Morning sickness can happen at any time of day, and mother said she experienced it right away. Most women don't but every pregnancy is different." He put his arm around her shoulders and held her close. "You did know you'd be having seven sons!"

"Well, certainly, but I didn't know it would happen this quickly!"

"In the line of the seven sons, all seven are usually born within ten years of marriage."

Her eyes widened. "That's a lot of babies really fast!"

"It is. May I settle your stomach. You'll probably need me to do it each day."

She nodded, and his hand moved to her abdomen. The nausea was gone in second. "Thank God that I'm married to a healer. I do not want to be sick every day for nine months."

"For most women, the nausea stops after the first three months, but for some it lasts the whole time. The babe is well."

"You could tell that?"

He nodded. "Tis a boy, of course. He will be born strong."

"Not if his mother throws him up!"

He laughed at that, pulling her closer. "You won't. I promise. It smells like the men have roasted the rabbits, and we can return to have supper. Do you think you can eat?"

She nodded. "My hunger has returned." She rested her head on his shoulder for a moment. "Thank you for understanding what I needed when I didn't."

He smiled kissing the top of her head. "I think you're the woman I've spent my whole life waiting for."

They slowly made their way back to camp, and then men looked at them curiously. They'd been gone a long time.

"You'll be happy to know that the next generation of McClain men are starting," Colin said with a grin.

After many congratulations, the rabbit was served, and they all ate, the men acting as if Brynna was unable to do anything on her own. Brynna didn't mind too terribly much, but she knew she would get tired of the treatment quickly. The journey must continue though, and she could endure it for the trip.

Days later, they reached their destination, and Colin followed the messenger into the keep, telling his men to guard his wife with their lives. A couple of the men looked offended that he would even feel the need to say it. They all knew their mistress was too important not to guard.

For Brynna the hour Colin was inside the keep felt like forever. She had no idea if they were treating him well or if he was being held prisoner. Finally, she reached out with her mind, "Is all well?"

The answer came to her swiftly. "Aye, all is well. There has been a sickness here, and I am treating many people. I will return soon."

She understood then why no one in Colin's traveling party was invited inside the keep. It was to keep them all from catching the illness. She visibly relaxed then, sitting on the ground outside the keep with her husband's men surrounding her.

When Colin finally came out of the keep, he looked exhausted. There were lines around his eyes that had never been there before, and he looked as if he had trouble standing. Without thinking, Brynna got to her feet and ran to him. "Are you all right?" she asked softly.

"There were many healings to do. We will head toward home now, but we must stop as soon as we are far enough from the keep. I don't want my enemy to know that healing weakens me so."

"I understand. Lean on me a little."

"You are too small. I would crush you with my weight."

"Just a little would be fine. Let's get to the horses, and we will ride away."

Colin's men saw how he leaned on his wife, but to anyone else looking, they would have thought it was affection for her. The men knew how his healing weakened him though. He tried to hide it, but they'd seen it too often to not understand what was happening.

All of them moved quickly, and Colin swung himself up onto his gelding without looking weak. Now it was simply getting to a spot far enough away for Colin to recover.

Colin led the group as the laird, and he rode swiftly away from the keep. Within a few minutes, he slowed, knowing they could no longer be seen. They camped just inside McPherson territory, though they wished it didn't have to be so.

The men helped Colin from his horse, while Brynna set up a place for him to sleep. He laughed softly as he watched her. "I'm not an Englishman. I don't need pillows and blankets to be comfortable. I can just wrap up in my plaid to sleep."

"Well, I'm an Englishwoman, and I would like to sleep beside my husband," she said, not caring as much about herself as she did about him. If he thought she was trying to get comfort for herself, she knew he would be more willing to sleep atop the bed she'd made.

He was asleep before supper was ready, and she woke him to eat a little, but then he went straight back to sleep. She snuggled against him before the sun was even down and covered them both. Summers were chilly in the Highlands.

Brynna fell asleep feeling content. She was with the man she loved, and she was having his child. A month ago, she'd have thought it was impossible, but now it seemed as if it had been her destiny all along. Colin was the man she was meant to be with. There was no doubt in her mind.

They traveled back to McClain land slower than they'd come. Colin healed Brynna twice per day so she wouldn't have to fight the terrible all day sickness that came with her pregnancy. She wasn't quite certain why anyone had ever called what she was experiencing morning sickness, because the feelings certainly didn't check the clock when they came on.

Finally, over two weeks after they left McClain land, they were home, and his mother was waiting at the keep for them.

"Did you tell her when we'd be home?" she asked Colin.

Colin nodded. "About an hour ago, I warned her that we'd be here about now. I knew she'd want to be here."

Holli hurried to them. "Are you both all right?"

Colin nodded. "The healing took a lot out of me because there were several people who were sick. That's why we're late. Besides, I didn't want to ride too quickly with my wife who is expecting."

Holli squealed and hugged Brynna close. "You hold the future of this family and this clan in the palm of your hands."

Brynna smiled. "I will be thrilled to have this babe and six more." She shook her head. "I certainly never thought I'd say that."

"Are you feeling all right?" Holli led them into the parlor, and they all sat.

"Thanks to Colin's twice daily healings I am. My stomach is not enjoying the babe's presence."

Holli nodded emphatically. "It was like that for me with all seven boys. But the daily healings really do help."

"I feel fine otherwise." Brynna shrugged. "I suppose it will be different when I'm big as the keep, but for now, I'm all right as long as Colin is close."

Holli looked at Colin. "You may need to send your brother on your healing trips til Brynna gives birth. Extreme morning sickness can make a woman waste down to nothing. I've even heard of it killing at times."

"I don't think it's that bad!" Brynna said, though she really wasn't sure. That first bout of sickness had taken her by surprise.

Colin nodded at his mother. "I do think it best if I stay with her until she's had the baby. Thankfully between my brothers, every power I have is duplicated."

"Oh, I had cook make a stew for supper. I hope that's acceptable," Holli said.

"As long as there are potatoes in the stew, I'll be quite happy. It's funny how I had never had them a month ago, and now I want them with each meal."

Holli laughed. "Of course there are! I ate baked potatoes every day while I was expecting. They calmed my stomach for whatever reason."

"Maybe I'll try them. So far the only thing calming mine is Colin."

"Well, I'm glad you're married to a healer then. Oh, I can't wait to share the news with the entire clan. Everyone will be so pleased that a babe is on the way."

"A wee bairn," Colin added with a laugh. "Mother has never been able to call her children bairns. They are always babies."

"Hey," Holli said, shaking her head. "I was born and raised in New York, not in Scotland."

"Tell me about New York. Do you have any books about it?" Brynna asked.

"I do actually. One of my favorite books is set in New York. I think reading about it will explain it much better than I ever could."

"I would enjoy borrowing that book."

"Well, I'm going to head out. I'll bring the book tomorrow. I need to serve my husband the supper I made."

Colin smiled. "Are you enjoying cooking every meal?"

"You know cooking has never been my favorite thing, but I'll do it. Your father deserves to eat and now that we're not laird and lady of the clan, we have no right to have meals prepared for us."

Brynna frowned. "You could take your meals here with Colin and me. I would enjoy that greatly!"

Holli shook her head. "No, you two deserve to have time alone together. The first year of marriage when you're learning all about each other is one of the greatest joys of life."

Colin laughed. "I have to wonder if Father would say the same."

"He would. He knows better than to disagree with me." Holli grinned as she headed to the keep's front door.

Brynna slumped a little when his mother was out of sight. "I think I'm going to get a bath after supper. All of my muscles are sore."

"I can take care of that for you, and then you can enjoy your bath, simply because you enjoy it and not to get rid of soreness."

"That sounds wonderful."

He put his hand on her shoulder and concentrated on healing her entire body. It was something he'd done often in his life, usually for the soldiers after training. "There. You should feel well now."

Brynna leaned toward him, putting her head on his shoulder. "Thank you. You're the best husband ever."

He chuckled. "We'll see if you feel that way in a few months when you're large with child."

"I'm going to guess right now that I will not feel this way. You should enjoy it while you have it."

He laughed. "I'm glad you can see our future so clearly."

"See? You're not the only one with gifts."

Chapter Nine

As the days went on, Brynna found that she relied on Colin for almost everything. After realizing how very much he did for her and everyone around them, she wanted to find a way that she could contribute other than just overseeing the keep.

While Colin was involved with his work one afternoon, Brynna walked out through the village to find Holli. The two of them spoke often, but there were usually people around, so it was hard to have real conversations.

Brynna found the cottage Colin's parents lived in after a bit of trial and error, and she knocked loudly on the door.

Holli opened the door and smiled when she saw Brynna. "Come in! Sit down! I have some cookies I baked the other day." Holli busied herself with bringing the cookies to the table. She also poured two glasses of milk. "To what do I owe the pleasure of this visit?"

Brynna sighed. "I feel like I'm useless." She reached for one of the cookies and bit into it. "Delicious!"

"I don't mind baking, but I'm not a fan of cooking at all." Holli tilted her head to one side, looking at Brynna. "Why do you feel useless?"

"Colin does everything. He works all day. Heals me often. He works so hard for us, and all I do is sit around and tell Cook what to fix for supper."

Holli smiled. "You're also doing something very important that Colin could never do."

At Brynna's blank look, Holli continued. "You're growing a human being. The first of seven sons. I remember when I was pregnant with my first. I felt like all I did was eat and nap. After he was born though, I knew my job was primarily motherhood. And then the next baby came, and the next. I spent so much time with my boys that I no longer felt like I wasn't doing my share. Finally, I felt like I was doing something important. I taught the boys right from wrong, made their clothes, and loved them. Now they're adults who are contributing members of our community."

Brynna bit her lip. "I suppose that will be true for me as well. But what can I do now to contribute to the world we live in."

"If growing your first son isn't enough, you should offer to watch children around the village. Then women would have a little time off, which we don't really get. Women have to cook seven days per week. They clean just as much. Only the men get Sundays off."

"I never thought of that. I will do that."

Holli smiled. "You could also spend a little time in the kitchen with Cook. In thirty years or so, you're going to be in a cottage in the village and not in the keep any longer, and Colin will still expect to eat."

"That's true. So I could help other women some days and work with Cook other days. Oh, thank you, Holli! I had no idea what I would do with myself for the next six months."

"When the baby arrives, there won't be any looking for things to do. You will simply take care of him and sleep when he does. It's a sobering experience being a new mom. We should find someone to help you with the babies actually. Seven in ten years is a lot for one woman to handle."

"Mayhap after the first I will need someone to help me. I'd like to try on my own with the first."

"I will ask around. It's best to find an older child, around twelve or thirteen. Because she will be with you for all the children, and you can train her without her thinking she already knows everything about children." Holli sighed. "I should have found a maid and companion for you when you first arrived."

"There was no need for one. There still isn't."

"Maybe you don't need a maid, but I think having a companion to do things with would help you a great deal. She could be with you when Colin has to leave for any reason, and she would be a friend to you. Someone you could talk to about anything."

"Did you have someone like that when you arrived?" Brynna asked.

Holli nodded. "I did. But more than that, my two best friends were here, and we were able to talk and enjoy one another's company. You came alone."

"I did. I thought I would make friends with all my new sisters and we'd spend time together, but that just hasn't happened for me. I wish it had."

"Yes, all of my daughters are busy with their own children. It was fun for those days they were with us though."

"It was fun. I wish we could do things like that more often."

Holli tilted her head to one side. "Perhaps we could. Not at night, but during the day. You could invite maybe three sisters at a time. And me. We could eat fun foods, let the children play together, and we women could read together or we could make some baby clothes. I have a feeling you're going to need some."

"I can't ask the other women to do my chores!"

"Of course you can. Everyone wants to help Lady McClain. We'd all sew and laugh together. It would be great fun for all because we wouldn't have to clean up any mess we made."

Brynna thought. "Mayhap we could do it on Wednesday every week. We do three sisters one week and three the next. And we let those coming decide what they want to do. If they want to sew, then we all sew. If they want to read together, we do that. Or if we want to make up a play to have the children perform, we could do that."

Holli laughed. "I like that last idea best. Am I invited both weeks?"

"Aye, of course you are."

They spent an hour at the table in Holli's cottage thinking of different things they could do. "And you hosting a party once a week still gives you time to learn from Cook."

"It would. Do all of the sisters like your Irish nachos and tacos?"

"Of course they do. If someone wants to marry one of my sons, I put them through the nacho test. If they don't like them, they need to find a different husband."

Brynna's eyes widened. "Really?"

Holli laughed. "Of course not. But they do all like them, and they would be thrilled to have them for lunch every other week."

"That's what we shall do then," Brynna said, smiling. "And the other days I'll learn from Cook." She got to her feet. "Thank you for the cookies and for the conversation. Now I have a purpose going forward."

Holli stood and walked Brynna to the door. "Thank you for coming to see me. I'm afraid I don't get a lot of visitors because people are used to me being in the keep and not in the village."

On her walk home, Brynna thought about everything Holli had said. There were ways for her to be helpful to others and learn what she needed to learn. She was certain all the sisters would love a day off of their chores. Perhaps she could send home a meal with each sister when they were with her. Then they wouldn't feel as though they needed to hurry home and make supper for their families. She'd have to talk to Cook about it.

When Brynna walked into the keep, she found Colin sitting at the table with all his brothers and his father. Instead of interrupting, she walked right past them to talk to Cook.

"Cook, I have a favor to ask of you."

Cook turned and smiled. "Aye, I'll do whatever you would like."

Brynna laughed. "You should hear what I'm asking for before you agree! I would like you to give me cooking lessons. Holli pointed out today that I will need to cook for Colin once my youngest son has married."

"Oh, I'd love to help with that. I suppose you want to learn about potatoes first and foremost." It obviously hadn't escaped Cook's attention that Brynna wanted potatoes with every meal.

"I think that would be lovely." Brynna reached out and hugged Cook. "Thank you so much!"

Cook smiled and patted Brynna's shoulder. "Tis my job to keep the lady of the keep in food. And if you want to learn, tis my job to teach you."

Brynna left the kitchen with a smile on her face and was almost to the table where Colin sat with his brothers and father when she remembered what she was going to do on Wednesdays. She turned on her heel and went straight back to the kitchen. "I forgot one thing."

Cook smiled her biggest smile. "Aye?"

"I forgot to tell you that I'm going to host Colin's mother and three of the sisters every Wednesday, as well as all the children." Brynna paused for a moment. "And if it's possible, I'd like to send supper home with all, so the women won't need to hurry out to cook for their families."

"I think that's a good way to get to know everyone. Aye, I can make meals for each family. Twill be the same as what I cook for you here."

"Perfect. Thank you!" Brynna hurried away and found her spot in the parlor. She'd long since given up needlepoint, but she'd begun sewing for the babe. She couldn't wait to hold her son in her arms, but she had six months to go still. And the all-day sickness had yet to fade away.

She stitched as she thought up different activities for her and her sisters to work on together. At times she worried that thinking of Colin's sisters as her own made her disloyal to her own sisters, but she never talked of it. She would miss all of her sisters, but especially Annie, the sister just older than she was. She and Annie had done everything together. Now, Annie was alone without her companionship. Writing a letter to let Annie know she was safe wasn't at all a good idea. Her father had never allowed any of his daughters to learn to read, though James, her younger brother, had been taught from the time he was small.

She glanced up as Colin walked into the parlor. "You were gone for a long while," he said, looking at her curiously.

"I went to visit your mother." She went on to explain everything that had been decided, and he smiled and nodded.

"I think that is a wonderful idea. You need to have time to spend with other women. You'll be overrun with boys soon enough." He sat down on the sofa beside her and looked at the gown she was making for the baby. "Your sewing improves every day."

Brynna looked down at the misshapen garment in her hands. "I don't want to think about how bad I was before then."

Colin hugged her to him. "You're the perfect wife for me," he said.

"You are an easy man to please." She set the garment down and turned to him. "Did you have a good meeting with your father and brothers?"

"Aye. I've been asked to heal another clan, but my brother is going instead. We were trying to decide who should accompany him, but Father is going to be one of those to go. He thinks it's better that one of the two of us should always go."

"I think you could go. I know your grandfather is here, and he could heal me."

"Nay. I will stay with my wife and heal her as needed. There's no reason to put the burden of healing on Grandfather. He is old, and he doesn't need to waste his energy that way."

"I hadn't thought of it that way. All right." Brynna sighed. "I would rather you were the only one healing me anyway, but I don't want people to think you are neglecting your duties for me."

Colin smiled. "No one thinks that. Everyone knows what the laird having seven sons means to this community. They all look at you with love, knowing you will be the one to bear those sons and keep the family line going."

Brynna yawned. "I can't believe how sleepy I get during the day."

"You're growing a person inside you. You need to eat for two and sleep for two."

"I'm just not sure it's possible for me to sleep that much and not feel lazy."

"You're anything but lazy. It's going to be all right. How's the stomach now? Do you think you can eat supper?"

"I don't. I will need your healing touch first."

"I'm always happy to touch my wife," he said, wiggling his eyebrows at her and causing her to giggle. When he put his hand on her belly and let the healing flow through her, she immediately felt better.

"I can eat now." Brynna smiled. "'Tis amazing what you can do with a mere touch."

"Let's go eat then." Colin got to his feet and offered her a hand.

While they ate, her mind was still going through all the activities she could do with the other McClain wives. She had many ideas, and they just kept coming.

"What are you thinking about?" Colin asked. Usually, they had lots to talk about during supper, but her mind was obviously somewhere else.

Brynna laughed. "I was just thinking about different things the sisters and your mother and I could do. I'm really looking forward to a day each week filled with activities." She shrugged. "All other days I'll be apprenticing under Cook. I need to be able to take care of our meals after our seventh son marries."

"We canna start talking about the seventh son before the first is even born."

She laughed. "I knew before we married I was expected to have seven sons. Why could we talk about it then and not now?"

He shrugged. "I think each child should be equally important. Not just the seventh. We should celebrate each boy as they come to us."

Brynna nodded. "You're right. We should. I'll try to focus on one at a time and being the best mother I can be."

"Good. That's how it should be."

"Your mother thinks we should find a companion for me. A maid who spends time with me all day."

"Maybe after the babe is born. I like the idea of you getting to know our sisters for now."

She smiled. "That's what I think as well."

Chapter Ten

The cooking lessons started the following day. Cook showed Brynna how to make simple baked potatoes. Brynna watched carefully, wanting to be able to make this for her husband someday. Then Cook showed her how to make a roast from pork and how to shred it to top the potatoes. The result was a glorious meal that Brynna felt as if she could make on her own the next time.

At supper, Colin said how much he loved the food, and Brynna smiled. "I helped make it. I think I could do it alone next time."

Colin grinned. "That's wonderful! I'm glad you're learning to cook."

"Me too. I didn't think it would ever happen."

"Would you like to walk after supper? It's staying light out late enough in the day that we could walk for an hour or two before it got dark."

Brynna took stock before nodding. "I think I could do that tonight."

"How have you been feeling today?"

"I'm doing much better than I have been. You said some women are only sick for the first three months they're expecting, and I'm hoping and praying that I'm one of those women."

On their walk around the loch, Brynna realized she was truly happy as a wife, now that she had a direction to go in. The only thing that kept her from being ecstatic was the fact Colin didn't love her.

As they walked and talked, he told her of his day and how his brother had communicated with him to let him know their healing party was on schedule and there had been no problems.

Brynna talked of learning to make the simple meal, and how excited she was to be able to do something that would really help them in the future.

They talked of the babe she carried and discussed name possibilities.

Brynna didn't know what made her ask the next question she asked, as it was completely out of character for her. "Why were you not married before we met?"

Colin shrugged. "I hadn't yet found a woman who I felt would be the one I needed to help me and be by my side through life."

"I see. I suppose you would still be unmarried if your mother hadn't asked if I wanted to stay and find a husband within your clan." She still became embarrassed when she thought about how she'd chosen the most important man to the future of the clan to be her husband, and had been so outspoken about it.

"Nay, I don't think that's true at all. I think you made it happen sooner than it would have, but by now we'd have been married, I'm certain."

"You are?" She looked at him with surprise.

"Of course. I would never have been able to be around you and not fall in love. I believe you were the person God created just for me."

She stopped walking, and he turned around when he realized she was no longer at his side. "Is something wrong?"

She felt the tears leaking out of the corner of her eyes as she stood still, staring at the man she loved with all her heart and soul. "I didn't think you'd ever fall in love with me!" Brynna wailed.

He walked back to her and put his arms around her, drawing her close. "How can you not realize the love I have for you?" He shook his head. "I tell you I love you every time I kiss you. Every time I make love with you. Every time I put your needs above those of the clan."

She looked up at him and blinked a few times to get the tears off her lashes. "I thought I was only a vessel for the sons you need. I didn't know you had feelings for the vessel."

"I wouldn't have married you had I not known I could fall in love with you. It happened at record speed; I must admit."

Brynna sighed happily. "I love you too, Colin."

"I know."

She shook her head. "How do you know?"

"How could I not? You do your best to be a good wife to me. You are willing to accept you will never have daughters as my wife. Everything about you screams to me that you love me, and I think everything about me screams it right back."

With his arm around her they continued walking. "I don't like the idea of any other man touching you to heal you. Not even my brother or grandfather. I see you and all I can think about is what a wonder it is that you came into my life. I want to thank the men who abducted you at the same time as I want to kill them. I never had confused thoughts like that until you came into my life."

Brynna sighed contentedly, realizing that his words had told her everything she needed to know. He loved her just as much as she loved him.

They walked in silence for a moment before she said, "I would like to send a messenger to my parents with a letter, so they know that I am well and married, and soon to be a mother. I think Mother will be relieved that I'm all right, while Father will be relieved he has to pay one less dowry."

"Do you want to travel to see them?"

Brynna thought about it for a moment before shaking her head. She had no desire to see her parents ever again. She just didn't want them to worry about her. Though she didn't think they did, she would make certain with her letter to them.

The following morning, the first thing she did after breaking her fast was to sit down and write a letter to her family. Her father and brother could read it to the rest of them.

Dear Family,

I am certain you realize that I was forcibly taken from the grounds of your home in the spring of this year. I was left tied to a tree when you wouldn't pay the ransom.

I want you to know that a loving man found me under that tree, and he made me his wife a few days later. I'm the wife of the Laird of Clan McClain. It is a good life I live, and I love my husband with all my heart. I am expecting our first child, and I pray that you are all doing as well as I am.

Please give my sister Annie my love and let her know she is welcome to visit here anytime. I live in the Highlands of Scotland now, and I feel as though my life is as perfect as a life can be.

I love you all,

Brynna McClain

When she was finished, she sealed the letter with a bit of wax and gave the letter to Colin. "Would you have a messenger take this to my family please?"

Colin nodded, reaching for her and pulling her onto his lap. "I will do it immediately. Will you be sad if there is no reply?"

Brynna shook her head. "No, I know my family didn't care for me as your family cares for you. It was not their way. This letter is for my own peace of mind, and truly nothing to do with them."

He smiled at her words, realizing she wouldn't be heartbroken even if her parents didn't acknowledge her letter.

Holding her close he smiled. "I plan to spend the rest of my life loving you. No one deserves to be treated as if they are unwanted, and I assure you, that part of your life is over. I love you with all my heart, Brynna McClain."

"And I love you, Colin McClain. Thank you for seeing more in me than my family ever did."

WHEN THE MESSENGER returned just shy of three months later, Brynna received a great surprise. With him, her sister stood smiling at her.

"Annie? You came!"

Annie laughed. "I asked Balloch if he was willing to bring me to you. Of course, halfway here, I realized I was in love with the man, and we found a priest to marry us."

Brynna got to her feet, her belly huge in front of her, hurried to her sister and hugged her close. "I bet Father was happy to be rid of us both."

Annie sighed. "Mother cried and cried until the letter came that you were well. Father said a daughter wasn't worth a penny of ransom unless she had a good match already made." She shook her head. "There are no girls left at home now, and Father couldn't be happier."

Brynna sighed. "And how is our brother?"

"He's to be married in one month. Father made sure we all knew that his upcoming marriage was a great deal more important than you being kidnapped and not found. Not that Father was willing to spare any knights to look for you. Mother begged and begged."

Brynna shook her head. "Well, I'm just happy that neither of us answer to our father any longer. And that you'll live in the village here. I'm so happy to see you, Annie!"

"As I am you. That journey felt like it took forever."

"I remember my journey into the Highlands with the kidnappers." Brynna shook her head. "Twas a miserable time, and I don't even know how many days passed." She took her sister's hand and led her to the dining area where Colin was having a meeting with his father. "Bryson, Colin, this is my sister Annie. She married Balloch, and has come to live in the village."

Colin smiled, getting to his feet and embracing Annie. "I know your presence here will bring Brynna great happiness. Thank you for coming."

Balloch had followed them into the dining area, and he nodded to Colin. "I couldn't leave my new wife in England with the horrible man she calls Father, now could I?"

Colin frowned. "What did he say when he received the message from Brynna?"

"The man started to shout and yell and throw things. He said a daughter of his should never have been taught to read, and he was disgusted with her." Balloch looked at Brynna for a moment before going on. "He said he never wanted to see her again, and when Annie said she wished to see her sister, he told her never to return. I already knew I loved her, so I didn't mind a bit."

Brynna smiled, though she felt a bit of pain at the news of her father's tantrum. "Tis as I expected. At least Mother knows I'm safe, and Annie is here with me. I couldn't have asked for more of the journey." She smiled at Balloch. "You'll both stay for supper tonight? I suppose you've discovered by now that Annie has no idea how to cook."

Balloch smiled. "I have realized that. I look forward to supper with you. Now, I'm taking my bride home, so she can see the small cottage she'll spend the rest of her days in."

"How could the size of the cottage matter?" Annie asked. "As long as I'm with the man I love and close to my sister, the world is a wonderful place."

"I couldn't agree more," Brynna said as Balloch walked away with her sister.

Brynna went back to the book she'd been reading in the parlor, quite happy her sister was there in the Highlands with her and loved by a man who would treat her well.

She rested her hand on the babe that grew within her, thinking what joy it would give her to introduce him to his Aunt Annie.

When Colin joined her a short while later, she was happily reading her book. "You are not upset with what your father said?"

"Nay. I live with the man I love, and I'm carrying his babe. My sister is here close to me, and we can see each other every day if we wish. I'm where I want to be." Brynna snuggled close to Colin. "Life couldn't get better."

Epilogue

Twelve years later, Brynna and Annie were walking with the children. Annie had three during those years while Brynna had all seven as expected. Thankfully Annie had girls so they weren't completely overrun with boys.

Annie carried her youngest, a babe of a mere six weeks, while Brynna held the hand of her youngest, three-year-old Duncan. Duncan had yet to share his power with his family if he had one at all. Brynna and Colin were certain the older boys had no powers as Colin's brothers had.

They were walking around the loch as they tried to do on fair days, and while they walked, Duncan looked at the water and said, "Rise up!"

Brynna looked at her son, and then at the water, which had formed into a pyramid. "Duncan, that's beautiful."

"Aye. I like the water."

"Can you do other things with water?" Brynna asked, wondering if her son had power over all water, or if he was controlling the wind to make it happen.

"Aye, Mama." With a flick of his wrist, Duncan froze the entire loch, and Brynna had to laugh. Her son had power over the water. She couldn't wait to tell Colin.

Annie had gotten used to seeing odd things when she was around the McClains, so she said nothing in response. Merely smiling at the way Brynna took her tiny boy having a power as a matter of fact.

"I can't wait to tell your papa!" Brynna said with a smile for her sister. "He's going to be so proud!"

Sign up for instant notification of all of Kirsten's New Releases http://www.kirstenandmorganna.com/newsletter